Pat

Hope you enjoy

first Novel.

Dr. Faust's List

Dr. Faust's List

Howard C. Humphrey

Pentland Press, Inc.
England • USA • Scotland

PUBLISHED BY PENTLAND PRESS, INC.
5122 Bur Oak Circle, Raleigh, North Carolina 27612
United States of America
919-782-0281

ISBN 1-57197-136-X
Library of Congress Catalog Card Number 98-067430

Printed in the United States of America

For Lee,
A promise kept.

Prologue

May 1540
Staufen Im Breisgau

The crowd was growing in both numbers and anxiety in the market square at the other end of Hauptstrasse. Hans Kopfel, from nearby Grunern, was passing around some of his fine homemade wines. In the Rathausplatz, just outside his window, Dr. Faust could hear the Burgermeister, Hermann Schmidt, trying to encourage the town council to go and intercept the mob.

Faust was absorbed in his experiment and was angry about the possible interruption. After all, Baron Anton von Staufen promised him when he recruited him to come to Staufen the previous year that he would have complete control, without interference, of everything.

The year was 1539 when the Baron was about to lose all his possessions. His silver mine was depleted and he was in serious debt to the moneylenders in Frieburg. The grape harvest was poor. He was in danger of being forced to sell the land around his castle. Land that had been in his family for six centuries. Land on which the town of Staufen im Breisgau was built.

That's when a former Heidelberg University classmate told him about Dr. Johannes Faust. A celebrated magician, astrologer, and alchemist who claimed he could turn base metals into gold. The Baron had him thoroughly investigated. He heard the tales of Faust's practice of the black arts, his penchant for beautiful young women, and of his supposed deal with Mephistopheles— the Devil, himself—to trade his soul for greater earthly pleasure and success. But the Baron was willing to gamble, and Faust needed a new sponsor. He also needed a new town, having been run out of Nuremberg, Ingolstadt, and Knittlingen.

Now, just a year later, he was on the very threshold of success. He had, at the baron's request, been installed in the Hotel Zum Lowen. It was the best in town. His room, number 5, was good, with space for his experiments and a fireplace to keep him warm and act as a receptacle for his notes from failed attempts.

He could now hear the crowd calling for him to be run out of Staufen. Some of them, no doubt, irate husbands of the ladies he had romanced. Others fearing his reported contacts with the Devil.

Just a little more time. He hid his notes in an oilcloth bag behind a loose stone inside the fireplace. "Almost finished," he thought, as he heard the screams getting louder. Then he heard pounding on the hotel's front door. He heard the Burgermeister calling for calm. "I must hurry," he said to himself, "I must finish." He could see the glow of torches playing on his first floor window above the front entrance. Then, as he heard the glass of the front door break, he poured the final compound too quickly.

To this day, no one is certain if it was the explosion that killed him or if he was murdered by the angry mob. His grave has never been found and he lives on more in legend and literature than in recorded history. The writings of Johannes Spies, Christopher Marlowe, and Johann Wolfgang von Goethe each romance the legend of Dr. Faust and the classic battle of good versus evil.

What is known, however, through the records of the Gasthaus Zum Lowen, is that room 5 on the second floor is frequently requested, even today.

Chapter 1

Monday, February 18, 1991
Day 1, Zurich

We had just checked into the Hotel Glarnischerhof in Zurich following a three week wintertime train and bus tour of Switzerland. Operation Desert Shield had begun shortly before we were to leave on our long planned vacation to Egypt. We decided to play it safe and travel to Switzerland instead. We were happy with that decision, as the bombing of Baghdad started five days before we left Boston to fly to Zurich. Perhaps it was our conservatism that caused all of what followed.

I had gone out on the balcony of our room and called to Lyn to come out and see the lake.

She said, "All right, Clark, where is it?"

"Here, Honey. Stand over here at this end of the balcony and look down that alley."

"Oh, I see it." she said facetiously.

"It's the Zurichsee," I said," Let's walk down there later. Maybe we can take a boat ride for cocktails."

"Sounds good, Dear." Then she pointed out that the back of another hotel was blocking most of our view. "Oh look at the sign, Clark, it's the Baur au Lac. I'd rather go there."

"That's the place where all the spies hang out in those adventure novels," I joked. "Let's go find one."

So, that evening we went to the Grill Room at the Baur au Lac looking for spies . . . and we found one.

The Grill Room was handsomely decorated in deeply carved dark wood and pieces of art. The table linens were crisp and the silver brightly polished. The service was very efficient. We ordered a bottle of Mumm's Cordon Rouge to celebrate the end of our vacation. It was Monday and we were scheduled to fly home on Thursday. At the waiter's urging, we ordered a first course of lentil soup with sausage, to be followed by the roast veal Zuricher with spaetzels.

Our soup course had just been served when the Grill Room door crashed open and a tall, slender man, complete with trench coat and hat, staggered into the room. He stumbled and fell on my back, his hat flying off. His head and arm slammed onto the table, spilling some soup, as he fell to the floor. Instinctively, I bent over him to see if he was okay. There was an enlarging blood stain on the front of his coat. He turned his head, looked up at me, and said, in a whisper, something that sounded like "Fau . . ." or "Faus . . ." Then he died.

As the patrons were screaming and running for the door, two other men pushed into the room. They came straight to our table, shoved me aside, and began searching the dead man's pockets. Not finding what they wanted, the smaller of the two—and they were both big, blonde, strong-arm types—grabbed me and shouted in German, "Wo ist die liste?" I knew just enough German to know he was looking for a list of something. I shrugged my shoulders to indicate that I didn't know anything. I was about to let them search me when the shrill of police sirens caused them to bolt out of the room through the kitchen.

I was regaining some composure when the police raced in. Some went in pursuit of the suspects while several others inspected the scene, examining the corpse and interviewing the other customers and staff. The detective in charge, after giving orders to the others, came to our table.

"Sit down, please," he said in perfect English. "The maître d'hôtel tells me you are American?"

"Yes, we're from Maine. Cape Elizabeth, Maine. I am Clark Keene and this is my wife, Lyn."

"Have you been long in Zurich?", he asked.

"We just arrived today," Lyn replied. "We have been touring Switzerland for the last three weeks."

"Ah, good. You liked our country?"

"Very much," we said together.

He introduced himself as Major Wilhelm Wallis, Chief Detective of Zurich's Homicide Division. He showed his credentials, smiled, and said, "Call me Willi, everyone does." Then he launched into what turned out to be a pleasant and surprisingly short interview. He asked if we knew the victim or knew either of the two men who searched him, if victim said anything or gave us anything, and would we come to police headquarters at 10:00 A.M. tomorrow to look at pictures to see if we could identify any of the three?"

I answered each in turn: "No. No. No. No," and "Yes." Only the third "No" was not completely true, but I had no idea what "Fau" meant.

After the police had gone into the lobby to question other witnesses, Lyn asked, "Are you still hungry?"

"No. Let's just go back to our room, have a stiff drink, and order room service." I did want to take a bite of the now cold soup, however, and as I raised my spoon, something caught my eye. Then I fished out of the soup a small key.

Once we were back in our room and had had two Dewars on the rocks, Lyn said, "Boy, when you said let's go look for spies, I never thought it would turn out like that. What do you think that was all about, Clark?"

"I don't have a clue, but I'll bet this key and 'Fau', whatever that is, have something to do with it."

"Yes, Dear, I'm sure of it. What do you think the key is for?"

"It looks like one of those locker keys they use in the train stations," I replied. "It's got a number on it. Number 657."

Lyn thought for a moment then said, "Should we give the key to that police official, Willi something, or should we try to find the locker?"

"We probably should give it to the police, Honey. But we said we wanted an adventure. Let's take a quick run by the Hauptbanhof in the morning. If we find anything we can take it to the police. It may contain a name or some other clue for them."

"Okay!" she exclaimed excitedly, "But do you think the killers will try to find us?"

"I don't know, Lyn, I don't know."

We finished the sandwiches room service had delivered and went to bed full of thoughts of spies dying in our arms, of thugs ready to torture us. And "Fau," or "Faus," and detectives and keys and lists.

Chapter 2

Monday, February 18
Day 1, Heiss Background

Rudi Heiss was not always a leader. As a boy he was small and suffered from allergies. His friends picked on him. The town bullies in Dresden beat him regularly. So when he was thirteen, he readily accepted the invitation from Klaus Faber to join his Aryan Elite gang. Klaus lived in his building, was nineteen, and had been gentle on those occasions when he fondled him in the basement. The gang was different.

Rudi learned self-defense and how to use guns, knives, and other instruments of death. He began to lift weights and study the writings and history of Adolph Hitler and the other leaders of the Nazi party.

By the time he was sixteen, he had killed eight people. Six of them silently, with his favorite weapon, an Italian stiletto. He kept it razor sharp. He played with it continuously, rolling it over and over in his hands.

His reputation for ruthlessness and his intelligence caused his rapid rise in the gang to leader of his neighborhood cell at eighteen. He took over the Dresden unit at nineteen in a bloody coup during which he personally executed "that pervert," Klaus.

The national organization sent him to Libya for terrorist training where he quickly demonstrated his proficiency in all forms of explosives. He was rapidly becoming the "wunderkind" of the Elite. Now, at twenty-two, he had been the leader of the Zurich cell for almost two years.

After dashing out through the kitchen entrance of the Baur au Lac, Rudi waited in the park across from the hotel's front entrance to further question the American and his wife.

He was watching when Major Wallis stationed several officers around the entrance. He decided to leave his partner, Peter Duren, to follow the Americans if they were not staying at the Baur. Peter reported that they left the hotel about twenty minutes after the incident, and that the police followed them, without being seen, one block up Bahnhofstrasse and then left one block to the Glarnischerhof. He also reported that he was able to take a picture of the couple with his infrared camera.

Rudi decided to wait until morning to try to isolate the Americans. He sent two of his group to watch the Glarnischerhof, and two to each the airport and the main train station. The picture Peter took wasn't the best, but it was good enough for recognition.

With that done, Rudi went to bed with thoughts of the list and the worm Dieder, who had died before he could get it from him . . . and the Americans, who, he had a strong feeling, knew more than their innocent appearance indicated.

"I will make them talk before they feel my stiletto," he thought.

Chapter 3

Tuesday, February 19
Day 2, Zurich

Lyn and I woke up early, still excited about the night before. We ordered room service, showered, and again planned our day. We would only look at the lockers at Hauptbanhof, the main train station. If the key didn't match, we would take it to Major Wallis. If it did match, we would take the contents to him. It might identify the owner and save us time looking at mug shots. After all, we still were on vacation.

"Isn't it a little strange," Lyn asked, "that the police did not quiz us more last night? Or offer us an escort back here?"

"Yes," I replied, "It is strange. I mean, those thugs could have been waiting for us outside the restaurant. I wonder if Willi, wasn't it, had us followed in the hope the killers would make contact."

"Hey, maybe they were both following us," Lyn suggested.

"You're probably right. They may still be watching us. I'll go down to the lobby and buy a *USA Today* and have a look around."

Our total experience with this sort of thing was limited to the forty adventure novels we read per year and my collection of James Bond videos.

"We are playing a very dangerous game, Clark, so be careful."

"I will."

After buying the paper, I stepped outside to check the weather, and even I couldn't help but notice the two men in dark suits jump up from their couch in the lobby and head for the door. Outside it was sunny but cold. I walked part way to the corner of the building. I saw two other men, not so well dressed, stiffen in their car seat across the street. So I quickly returned to the hotel. As I got on the elevator, I saw the two "suits" return to their sofa.

Once back in the room, I exclaimed, "You were right. It appears we have two policemen in the lobby and two bad guys in a car on the street."

"What should we do, Clark? Should we just take the key to the police? We could ask the two in the lobby to take us."

"No. What if I'm wrong about which are the police. Let's see if we can get out of the hotel without being seen. If we can, we'll go ahead as planned."

"Okay. I'm not sure how much of this spy stuff I want, but it sure is exciting."

We finished breakfast, read that the Chicago Bulls had beaten our Celtics again, and got ready to leave. We decided to take our travel shoulder bag with us, as it contained all our valuables, tickets, and cash. We would stop by the TWA office later to confirm our flight to Boston for Thursday.

I put the locker key in my jacket pocket . We found the service elevator and took it to the ground floor. We were in a back hall. There was a door to the kitchen, one into the lobby, and one down a hall marked exit. The latter door led into a trash collection area in the alley. We went out and, seeing no one, we went two blocks away from the Limmat River and Bahnhofstrasse, and then circled our way around to the station. We were sure we weren't followed. We had almost walked all the way backwards, we were so nervous.

In the station we went to the first set of lockers. Number 657, wasn't in that section, but the keys in the empty lockers matched the one we had. We finally found 657 near the trains. We cautiously opened the locker and removed a small canvas pouch.

"Let's sit over there on that bench and have a look at what was so important to our spy," I said.

Lyn grabbed the pouch and crossed rapidly to the bench without an answer. When seated, she opened the pouch and removed two items. An old notebook like students use and a single piece of paper with six names . . . no doubt the killers' "liste."

As we started to rise, we could see two leather clad blondes looking up and down at a picture and at us. Then they started walking very fast in our direction. We ran out along the train platform. A train was pulling out on our track. It was gaining momentum, but the doors were still open. I pushed Lyn on and jumped on behind her just as the doors closed. I looked back and could see our pursuers checking the monitor to see where our train was headed.

They knew more than we did. We still had our Eurrail passes in the travel bag and they were good for twelve more days. I found the conductor and learned we were on our way to Basle. By the time I returned, Lyn had found seats in an empty compartment and she was studying the list.

"This does not mean much to me," she said pushing it forward. It read:

DV	Msgr. Ricardo Corso	Rome
F	Gunter Siegrist	Staufen
G	Prof. Ernst Schnelling	Heidelberg
M	Gaspar Catalbo	Palermo
S	Countess Liesel Anton	Corfu
US	Kermit Blackmann	Boulder

"No, it doesn't mean much to me either. If we knew what the letters stood for, then, maybe."

"The notebook might help," she said.

"Yes, but first let's figure out what we are going to do. We need to go somewhere that we won't be found by these tough looking thugs."

Lyn added, "And what are we going to do about the police? Willi is sure going to be mad at us."

"They will check our room and start looking for us when we don't show up this morning," I replied.

"That may be the best thing, Dear."

"We should get off this train before it gets to Basle. That's a big town and the bad guys may have people waiting."

The train was pulling into Olten, an industrial town at the crossroads of the route from Zurich to Basle or Bern. Without talking, we both got up and got off the train. There were very few people around the station, as it wasn't yet tourist season. We crossed the street and sat by the window of a small cafe. After ordering tea for me, hot chocolate for Lyn, and fresh baked rolls for both of us, we opened the notebook. It was in German. We could make out a few words, but most of it was formulas, drawings, and what appeared to be chemical compounds.

"Look," said Lyn, "here's a name I've heard . . . Faust . . . Dr. Johann Faust."

"That could be what the victim was trying to say to me last night. Faust. Did not he have something to do with the devil?"

"He is a character in a play we had to read in college. It was all about good versus evil. By Goethe, I think."

"I remember. He was a sorcerer who tried to make gold out of other metals. That's probably what all these formulas are about."

"No one ever actually did that, did they, Clark?"

"I don't think so. But the guys chasing us must think so. This 'F' on the list could represent Faust."

"Then this Gunter Siegrist in Staufen must know something," Lyn added. "Where is Staufen?"

I confessed I had no idea, though I fancy myself a geography expert.

We kept studying the notebook and decided Monsignor Corso's "DV" could be DaVinci. His name was in the notebook. The "S" by Countess Anton could again refer to Staufen. But, why? Professor Schnelling's "G" we weren't sure about. It could be for gold. We found a few "M" words including Mafioso, and we were fairly certain the "US" simply stood for the United States. There were two company names near Mr. Blackmann's. They were Denver Mining and Homestead Mines, both of which I knew had interests in gold mining.

"This is really getting interesting. Can we check with the people on this list to see what they know, Clark?"

"I think it's too dangerous, Lyn. After all, the people chasing us have already killed one man to get this list. And for a retired life insurance salesman and a retired teacher from Maine, we do not have the training or the skills to stay ahead of them."

"Oh Clark, we've done pretty well so far. We can just outsmart them."

"No, Lyn, there are too many of them and they obviously have a communications system. I'm calling Major Wallis."

I went outside to a phone booth and dialed the number Major Wallis had given us. He answered it himself on the first ring, so it must have been his private line.

"Ja?" he answered.

"Major, it's me. The American, Clark Keene."

"Where are you?" he shouted in English. "What is going on here? Why did you sneak out of the hotel?"

"We can explain. We are at the train station in Olten. We are being chased by some very tough looking people. We found a locker key after you left last night and went to the main station in Zurich this morning to see what was there so we could bring it to you," I rambled on nervously.

"You have this with you?"

"Yes."

"Gut. I'll send police to bring you back."

"I don't know, Major, these people seem very resourceful. They may have people here."

"Okay, you wait. I'll come myself. Only forty-five minutes."

"Thank you, Willi. We will wait here for you." Abruptly, he hung up. At the same moment, in Major Wallis outer office, another phone was hung up, picked up, and re-dialed.

"Rudi, it is Ulrich Hurd. They are at the train station in Olten waiting for the major."

"Good work Ulrich. We'll take care of it. I'll put your money in the usual place." Then Rudi Heiss dialed a cellular number to reach Jens Baer and Heinz Ruppert, who were in the car from the Glarnischerhof, now on the road to Basle. They planned to pick up the Americans from their team in Basle and take them back to Rudi.

"We are just five kilometers past Olten now, Rudi. We'll turn around and be there in ten minutes."

"Gut, Jens, call me when you have them."

"Ja. Out."

We decided we would stay at the cafe and watch. We also surveyed alternate escape routes just in case. There was a Eurocar rental agency next door to the cafe. I verified they had cars available and even had them start the paper work on a BMW. We didn't plan to use it, but just minutes later we rushed back into their office.

The car I had seen at the hotel that morning came screeching to a stop in front of the station and two leather clad thugs jumped out of it and ran into the building. That's when we ran next door, finished the rental agreement and went out the back way into their lot. We exited the lot into the alley and worked our way to the N1 headed for Bern.

"My God, Lyn, how did they get there so fast?"

"And how did they know where to find us, Clark? There must be a leak in Willi's office. And, I suppose, they could have been on their way to Basle trying to catch up to us." She was answering her own questions.

"Well, it looks like you get your way, Lyn. We're in this thing whether we like it or not. So, where on the list do you want to go first?"

"I vote for Rome," she said, "I'll feel a lot safer out of Switzerland."

"Or Germany for that matter," I added.

So we settled on driving to Bern. There we might be able to catch an overnight train to Rome. Fortunately, that morning we had taken our travel bag which contained our passports, Eurrail passes, travelers checks, credit cards, cash, and other valuables. We could call the Glarnischerhof and ask them to store our clothes. We would buy what we needed in Bern.

My mind was racing when Lyn exclaimed, "This is fun!"

Back at Olten, both the bad guys and Willi had separately discovered that we had rented the BMW. We had used a credit card, so they had our name. Willi also learned someone had been there before him.

He asked himself the same questions we had. "How did they know where to go?" and "How did they get there so fast?" His answers were also the same.

Rudi was not pleased when he heard we had evaded capture again. He had Peter Duren's picture of us faxed to all their cells. Willi issued an all points bulletin, with a description of the car, to detain us.

Reluctantly, Rudi placed a call to Berlin. He called the national leader of the Aryan Elite, Max Bormann. As smart and as vicious as his grandfather Martin, who had served Hitler as his chief of staff. "You have two days, Rudi. Find them, or else."

Chapter 4

The reverberations of Rudi's call to Berlin were nearly world wide.

In Langley, Virginia, at the CIA's European Terrorist Center, Assistant Director Brendan Howard was reviewing the transmissions report from the previous night. His wire room supervisor, Cathy Pagent, entered his office and said, "Did you see the entry on that report for the Aryan Elite Zurich to Berlin call?"

"Not yet, Cathy."

"Well it looks like they're getting active. Here is the full text of the transmission. This Rudi Heiss, in Zurich is chasing some American couple who has taken their list of something from them."

"What's the list about?"

"We do not know, but the call was to Max Bormann and he got excited. He gave this Rudi a 'find them in two days, or else' command."

"Have you checked on whether they are our operatives?"

"No, Brendan, I just got the text."

Brendan picked up his phone and called his counterpart in European Covert Operations, Bryan Roberts. "Mr. Roberts office. This is his aide, Allyson Lee."

"Hi Ally, it's Brendan. Is he in yet?"

"He's here. Just a minute, Brendan, he's right down the hall. I'll get him. Are we still on for tonight?"

"Yes, I'll pick you up at 7:00. We can get a bite at the Old Ebbit. The game's at 8:30."

After two stanzas of Nat King Cole's "Unforgettable" played on the hold line, Bryan's big voice boomed, "Hey Brendan, did you call to invite me to the hockey game tonight?"

"No, Bryan, I'm taking Allyson. She is a lot prettier than you. I called to see if you have an op going in Switzerland against the Aryan Elite?"

"No. They've been quiet."

"Well, Cathy Pagent picked up a call from Zurich to Bormann in Berlin. They are apparently trying to find an American couple who stole a list of something from them. They sound desperate as Bormann gave this Rudi a 'two days, or else' order."

"That would be Rudi Heiss. He's their Zurich chief and a real bad character, Brendan. Send the transcript over and I'll put our Swiss operative, Ridley Taylor, on it."

"Okay, Bryan."

"Sure you don't have a ticket for me tonight? The Caps are playing the Blues."

"Not tonight. And thanks."

In Baghdad, General Mahmoud Hanfi entered Saddam Hussein's underground office. Even though he was the head of Hussein's secret service, he had been thoroughly searched and forced to leave his weapon with the palace guard before entering. "I have news which may be of interest from our man in Zurich, your Excellency."

"What is it?" Saddam barked as he looked up from the papers on his desk.

"Yousef Mohammed learned from his police informant that the Germans think they have found the list for making gold."

"Ah ha! To have such a thing, Mahmoud. To be able to manufacture gold. We could win easily this war with the infidel Bush and his puppet coalition. We could control the world's financial markets and ruin their economy. I must have this list."

"Yes, your Excellency, I knew you would be pleased."

"Take Seraph Najim. Take her and two of her assassin team and join Yousef in the hunt. You must not fail!"

"Yes, your Excellency."

At that same moment in Sicily, Gaspar Catalbo was on his way from Palermo into the mountains to Corleone. He needed to tell the Don that a list of gold had surfaced in Zurich. Vittorio had received a call from his confidant, Ulrich, that some Americans named Keene had the list. Both the police and the Aryan Elite were looking for them. The Don would be pleased that Vittorio had already put out the word to watch for the Americans and to get the list. Yes, Gaspar knew the Don would be pleased.

It was before 6 A.M., in Denver, when Kermit Blackmann's phone jangled him awake. "Mr. Blackmann, it is Ulrich Hurd, from Zurich. You promised a reward if I ever heard about a list of gold," the voice on the other end boomed.

"Yes," exclaimed Kermit, now wide awake. "What has happened?"

"The group who call themselves the Aryan Elite killed your agent, Dieder Swartzbach, because they thought he had such a list. Now they are chasing an American couple who they think got it from Dieder."

"They're not ours, Ulrich. I didn't even know Dieder had found such a list. He probably was going to try to sell it to us for more money. But thank you, Ulrich. I'll wire your reward in the morning. Pleased keep me informed."

When he hung up, Kermit Blackmann dialed his boss Dan Adams, C.E.O. of Denver Mining. "May not be anything, Danny, but it looks like that stupid list about people making gold has surfaced again. This time in Switzerland. They say that some Americans named Keene have it, and the police, the Germans, and Lord knows who else are after them."

"Well, I don't have to tell you, Kerm, that if such a thing really works, we are out of business. All those lovely stock options the shareholders granted you as our General Counsel will be worthless."

"Right."

"Get on it, Kerm, and try to keep it under wraps. I'll call Kerry James over at Homestead and fill her in. You get ready to go. Plan to leave in three hours in case she wants to send someone with you."

"Okay, boss."

✤ ✤ ✤ ✤ ✤ ✤

So, without knowing all this was going on . . . that the hunt was gaining more dangerous players . . . Clark and Lyn Keene were still on the N1 nearing Bern.

"We really are going to be all right, aren't we Clark?"

"I hope so, Dear, I hope so."

Chapter 5

Tuesday, February 19
Day 2, Switzerland

Lyn had been silent for a while, obviously thinking about our situation. I had been thinking, too, about what our pursuers might be doing. At the same moment, both of us said, "Do you think there will be people waiting for us in Bern?" We laughed to relieve the tension.

"There well could be," I volunteered. "The police probably know we rented this car. And they could issue an all points bulletin, or whatever they call it over here."

"Yes, and those other people seem to have agents everywhere. What can we do, Clark?"

"Well, we used our own credit card to rent this car. They're, no doubt, looking for it and watching the turn in offices."

"Didn't you tell Eurocar we were going to turn it in at the Lucerne station?"

"Yes, but they won't believe that. In fact, it's probably not a good idea to be out on this major highway. They know this is one of the main roads from Olten."

"And they know it goes to Bern," Lyn added nervously.

"Look at that map the car company gave us, Honey. Are there any cutoffs coming up before we get into the city?"

"Here's one. Just before Bern the N6 goes south toward Interlaken," she said, pointing to the map.

"That's it!" I exclaimed. "We can leave the car in Thun on the street. I'll call Eurocar and tell them where they can find it. Then we can take a train or the boat to Spiez, and change to the train over the Falsenberg pass to Brig."

"Oh yes, Clark. Then we could go up to Zermatt and hole up with Frank and Fran."

"Sounds good, Hon. Watch for the cutoff."

Just as we entered the interchange, we could see a police helicopter coming up the highway from Bern. We paused under an overpass and the chopper continued up the highway towards Olten.

As we were pulling back on to the highway a small Renault pulled up even with us. The window was lowered and a tough looking character waived a .45 caliber pistol and motioned for us to pull over. Instead, I jammed on the accelerator and the BMW shot forward with one bullet breaking the back seat window behind me and a second lodging itself in the trunk.

"Hurry, Clark!"

"I am. That Renault should be no match for this car."

We were doing 175 kilometers per hour and continued to put distance between us and the gunman. When they were out of sight, we turned off the highway and took the back roads toward Thun. We parked the car in a restaurant parking lot on the edge of the city, leaving the keys on the visor. Then we caught a local bus which took us straight to the ship station. We felt the boat would be less likely to be watched than the trains.

As we were buying tickets, Lyn cried, "I'm scared. That man was shooting at us!"

"We need to go low profile. Turn your coat collar up and put on your sunglasses," I urged.

"I'll feel better when we get to Beaver and Fran's," she muttered.

We had been in Zermatt ten days before, skiing with our good friends, Frank and Fran Schultz. "Beaver," as we called him, had built their chalet two years before and had been after us to visit them. The house was beautifully situated at the base of the Gornergrat at the south end of Zermatt, with magnificent views of the Materhorn. Beaver was one of the top salesmen for the same company I had sold for. They were from a small town in Illinois and we used to see them each year at the company conventions. Skiing was a shared passion for the four of us. It was easy for us in Maine to get to the slopes. But there aren't many near Illinois, so they had traveled to all the great ski resorts and decided on Zermatt as the place for their winter getaways . . . we sure couldn't fault their choice. While we were with them earlier in the month, the skiing had been outstanding. They had shown us all the runs. Even one over the top and down into Cervinia, Italy.

"They'll be surprised to see us," Lyn said. "With Beaver's fluent German, maybe he can help us with the notebook."

"Yes, and they can help us get some clothes. Let's go there and hide for a few days while this all settles down."

Ten minutes later we were on a local Thunersee passenger boat on our way to Spiez. The boat landing at Spiez, we knew, was below the train station. It is small and we didn't see anyone lurking about as we waited in the bar for the train to Brig.

Brig is a much larger town and we imagined every other traveler was looking at us. Upon our arrival at Brig we ran from the regular station to the end where the trains to Zermatt depart. The train pulled out just after we boarded. I looked back and thought I saw someone running around the corner of the station trying to catch our train. He missed it, and for the moment we were safe.

The off-duty Brig policeman thought we were someone he had seen a bulletin about so he went back to headquarters to look at the files. He finally found a bulletin in the stack of new papers where the descriptions matched. It was a couple named Keene who were being sought by a Major Wallis in Zurich. He called the number on the bulletin. The major had returned from Olten, and had searched our room at the Glarnischerhof. He had just finished impounding our luggage and clothes and was walking back into his office when the phone rang.

"My name is Markel, sir. I am a patrolman from Brig, and I may have seen the couple you seek."

"In Brig? Were they headed toward Italy?"

"No. They got on the train going to Zermatt."

"Are you sure it is them?"

"No, but they match your description and they were in city clothes."

"It's probably them. Their rental car was found in Thun, so they could have been on the way there. Thank you, Officer Markel. I'll take it from here."

The major hung up and called Ulrich Hurd into his office. "Ulrich, arrange for our police helicopter to fly me to Zermatt. It seems the Keenes have gone there. And call the Chief of police there and tell him to meet me at 9:00. We'll have to land in the large parking lot at Tasch." Then the major went by his apartment to pack.

After arranging for the helicopter, Ulrich called the police station in Zermatt. "Our Chief is up on the ski slopes helping to wind up the day," the voice answered.

"Please tell him Major Wallis, Chief of Detectives from Zurich, will arrive by helicopter at the parking lot in Tasch at 9:00 tonight."

"I'll tell him."

When Ulrich finished that call, he started to think of all the money he was going to make—enough to take his beautiful Sonja to Nice. Oh, how lovely she looked in her swim suit. Even better with it off in bed! Perhaps he would earn enough to ask her to marry him. He was licking his lips as he dialed the first of the four calls he would make to Rudi, Vittorio, Yousef, and Mr. Blackmann. They all paid well.

The mountains make their own weather and the afternoon clouds were beginning to gather over the Alps, foreboding danger ahead.

Chapter 6

Tuesday, February 19
Day 2, Zermatt

The ride up the Mattertal Gorge is one of the most scenic rail trips in the world. Lyn and I had taken the ride to Zermatt seven or eight times. Each time it seemed more beautiful. It was unseasonably warm for February and the snow melt was forcing the waterfalls and the stream to carry a much larger volume of water than when we were there just two weeks ago. But there was still plenty of snow on the peaks. There were hordes of skiers at the stations at St. Niklaus, Randa, and Tasch, where they left their cars in the large parking lots. No cars are permitted in Zermatt.

By the time we arrived in Zermatt, the train was over-full, with people standing in the aisles. Almost everyone was carrying skis, boots, and their back packs. Even though it was midweek, Zermatt was going to be full.

We tried to melt in with the crowd as we flowed out of the station onto the main street. There were electric hotel carts meeting the train to haul the skis and luggage. Except for those who needed assistance, everyone began to trudge up the street to their lodging.

As we climbed higher, we lost both carts and walkers to the side streets and hotels. By the time we reached the turnoff to the path to Beaver and Fran's place, we were alone. We stopped at the last terraced stube by the cable car station. We had a beer while we watched to see if we had been followed. No one came up as far as the lift.

After fifteen minutes of watching, we went on up the path to our friends chalet and knocked on the door. The lights came on in the main room and Fran answered the door. A look of amazement spread over her face as she screamed, "What are you doing here?"

"It's a long story," Lyn replied, "We need help. We're being chased and need to hide out for a few days."

Beaver had entered the great-room from the kitchen uttering, "Being chased. Hide out. What the hell is going on?"

"But first come in," Fran said, "It must be cold out there in those city clothes. Of course you can stay."

"Where are your clothes?" Beaver asked, continuing his inquisition.

"You won't believe what's happened to us," I started, "But if you still have some of that Chivas Regal, we'll tell you all about it."

With another log on the fire and the drinks served, we started with our arrival in Zurich, the idea of looking for spies at the Baur au Lac, the murder, the ruffians, the police, finding the key, and then finding the locker after sneaking out of the hotel. Then Lyn covered the chase to and from Olten, abandoning the car in Thun, and our trip to Zermatt. We were both talking so fast and interrupting each other so often, it's surprising they understood anything.

"Why didn't you just go to the police?" Beaver wanted to know.

"What was in the locker?" was Fran's question.

"We tried to turn ourselves in to the police, but the bad guys showed up in Olten just minutes after I called the head man's private number."

"Ouch!" was Beaver's response.

"Here," said Lyn, as she was digging in our travel bag. She handed the notebook and the list to Beaver. "Here's what was in the locker. This list of names and places, and this notebook that is written in German."

"We thought you may be able to read it for us, Beav," I added.

"Let me see. It's in German all right. But it's formal German like they use in the universities. I'm not sure how much I can read, but I'll give it a try tonight."

Fran rose and took Lyn to the kitchen, saying, "Of course you can stay as long as you like. Come help me expand the beef and noodles I was fixing for supper."

Once they were gone, I admitted to Beaver that I was really frightened, particularly for Lyn.

"We sure don't want to get you in any trouble."

"Don't worry about us," Beaver replied, "You are safe here." He then started to puzzle over the notebook. I took a pen and a tablet as I always did when I had a big problem. I drew two lines down the page to make three columns. Above the left third of the page I wrote "Options," in the middle the word "Plus," and on the right, "Minus." Then, under "OPTIONS" I listed:

> Call Major Wallis again
>
> Continue on to Rome
>
> Call the U.S. Embassy
>
> Leave the list and notebook
> with the local police
>
> Fly home

The girls cooked and resumed their conversation from days before as if we had never left. Beaver read and said a lot of "Uh Huhs" and "Ums." I drank the Chivas and thought about the options. The dinner was excellent. I showed the options list to Lyn. We decided to sleep on it, as we were exhausted. We went to bed early, leaving our friends laboring over the notebook and the list. My last thought as I fell asleep was that this all began only last night. It was hard work being a spy.

Chapter 7

Tuesday, February 19
Day 2, Zermatt

Chief Bruno Mueller was waiting for Major Wallis's helicopter as it touched down in the far end of the large parking lot at Tasch. It was almost 9:00, but the full moon on the snow made it seem like daytime.

"I'm Bruno Mueller, Major. My men are all waiting at our headquarters. We can take our Land Rover, one of the few vehicles allowed in Zermatt."

"Thank you for your cooperation Chief Mueller. I'll wait and brief you all when we get there. And, please call me Willi, everyone does."

"We are not very formal here either. All my men and the townspeople call me Bruno."

When they arrived at the police station about fifteen minutes later, the entire police force of eight officers, including the chief, were assembled in the outer room of the two room building.

"This is Major Wilhelm Wallis, Chief of Detectives in Zurich." Bruno continued with the introductions of his men, which included one woman who led their ski patrol.

"Call me Willi, please. We have a situation where we think two Americans arrived in Zermatt this evening. They have innocently come into certain documents, including a list, that some very nasty people who call themselves the Aryan Elite want. This group has chased them across Switzerland today. They seem to have a pipeline into my office as they have been ahead of me all day."

"The Americans, a couple named Clark and Lyn Keene, called me earlier to pick them up in Olten. Somehow this neo-nazi group got there first. So the Keenes are obviously afraid to call again. I'm working on the leak in my office. I only told one of my men I was coming here."

It is important that we find the Keenes first. Here is a description of them, including the clothes they were wearing when they rented a car in Olten. Here also are their passport numbers and the credit card number they used to rent the car. They are not dangerous, but I'm sure they are frightened. They need to be brought to me."

Bruno passed out the descriptions and sent everyone out to check the hotels and guest houses to see if they were registered. About 11:00 the final report came in. All were negative. Then they began to survey the restaurants and bars to see if anyone had seen them. After another two hours, the reports were again negative, with one exception.

A waiter at the Waliserhof Weinstube told the police he thought they sounded like a couple that had eaten there several times a few weeks ago. "They were always with another couple who come here often. I don't know their name, but the man they called some animal name . . . like Marmot, or Woodchuck . . . no, wait, it was Beaver. That's it. They all called him Beaver."

Willi said, "Well that's something. Sounds like in the morning we're going to go Beaver hunting."

"I can only spare four of us tomorrow, Willi. It will be a very busy day on the slopes."

"That should be enough, Bruno. Could you take a local map and mark off all the houses where you know the occupants. Now, let's get some sleep."

"Report back at 8 A.M. Jan you take the A squad to cover the skiing. The B squad will do the house to house canvass," Bruno said as he closed the meeting.

Rudi Heiss, Jens Baer, and Heinz Ruppert had arrived by car in Tasch at 10:00. They took rooms in a gasthaus there. The trains had stopped running to Zermatt, so they borrowed some cross country skis from the gasthaus owner to ski to Zermatt for the "night life."

"Be careful," the owner said. "I'll leave the front door unlocked for you."

"Danke! We'll be careful," Rudi answered. They skied up the service road in a little under twenty-five minutes. They stored their skis in the rental racks at the train station and began to check the bars. They soon saw the local police were doing the same. Rudi decided they should simply watch police headquarters to see if any activity developed. He was sure that was the correct course of action when he saw Major Wallis through the window. He knew if he followed him, Willi would lead them to the Americans.

It was a little after 1:00 when the officers all went home to sleep. The major and the local who seemed to be in charge went into the back room to sleep on cots.

"Let's take shifts. Jens, you first. Watch the building and if Wallis comes out, call me on the cellular phone. Heinz will replace you at 4:00, and I will take over at 7:00. Then I want you both back on the 8:30 train in the morning. We'll take the extra set of skis back so our landlord won't become suspicious."

Rudi was certain nothing would happen until tomorrow. He wanted to be fresh for whatever the day might bring. He skied back to Tasch and as he lay down to sleep, he knew he would see the American couple in the morning. He would make them talk. Then they would feel the sting of his stiletto.

Chapter 8

Wednesday, February 20
Day 3, Various

Kermit Blackmann and Ned O'Brien were in the Citation over the Atlantic when the call came from his secretary saying someone named Ulrich had called and said Zermatt.

"Thanks, Norma, that's where we'll be going. See if you can get me a suite at the Mt. Cervin. Two bedrooms for Ned O'Brien, from Homestead Mines, and me. And get rooms for the pilots in Visp or Brig. We'll land at Visp and take the train up."

✢ ✢ ✢ ✢ ✢ ✢

Gaspar's meeting with the Don had gone well. The Don reminded him that the family had done it's own experiments over the last two centuries without success.

"You can't get gold from lead, Gaspar," he joked. "You can steal it if the lead is a bullet in a gun!" The Don laughed at his good one. Gaspar laughed, too. "But, who knows? Maybe this time it's different. The potential gain from such a thing is immense. We could control everything. Kings and Governments would bend to our wishes. Yes, if it exists, we must have it. Tell Vittorio we are sending Anthony Ruffini to help." Tony Ruffini was the Don's number one enforcer.

Early the next morning, Tony and Gaspar were having breakfast at Gaspar's Bar. Vittorio called to say the couple had gone to Zermatt. So instead of the scheduled flight to Zurich, Gaspar took Tony to the charter service at Palermo's airport where they arranged for a flight to Visp. They had told Vittorio to pick him up there around 9:30.

Mamoud Hanfi, along with Seraph Najim and her two assassins had arrived in Zurich at 6:30 A.M. on the Emirates Air night flight from Amman, Jordan. When Yousef met them, he had rented a nine passenger Fiat Ducato. They left immediately for the drive to Zermatt.

Ridley Taylor, the CIA Chief of Station in Bern, was packing to leave early and drive to Zurich. Just before he left, Cathy Pagent called from Washington, at 1 A.M. her time.

"We have a report from the air traffic section that a plane belonging to Denver Mining changed their flight plan over the Atlantic. They asked to be switched from Zurich to Visp."

"That's the airport that is closest to Zermatt, Cath. Sounds like I may have company."

"You sure will, Ridley. The Swiss police issued an all points and they are in the hunt. Also, we know this neo-nazi group, the Aryan Elite is on their trail. We also suspect the Iraqis may be onto it too. There was phone traffic between Zurich and Baghdad last night . . . plus, General Hanfi, along with three of Hussein's assassins, was on an Emirates Air flight from Amman to Zurich early this morning. Don't know of others, but there may be some."

"That's enough. Tell our Mr. Roberts that I'm on my way to Visp to pick up the trail. I'll call him when I have news."

When Cathy called Bryan Roberts at home to give him this new information, he decided, with Iraq now involved, it was time to inform the President. He called William Webster, the director of the agency and briefed him on the affair. When he heard of the possible involvement of Iraq, he agreed the President must be told.

He asked Bryan to bring Cathy and Brendan Howard to his office at 7:00 to fully brief him and to discuss options. He then called the President to set up a meeting, suggesting that the Secretaries of Defense and Treasury should attend.

President Bush decided that in addition to Nicolas Brady and Dick Cheney, he would have the Chairman of the Joint Chiefs, Colin Powell, and Secretary of State James Baker attend. The meeting was set for 10:00 Thursday morning, as Cheney and Powell were in Ridyah, Saudi Arabia conferring with Schwarzkopf.

That morning in Switzerland brought bright sunshine, a cloudless sky, and gorgeous views of the Materhorn. The air was clean and crisp, but not too cold. About two degrees centigrade, thirty-five or so Fahrenheit. The morning also brought scenes that could have been in a funny spy spoof movie.

Denver Mining's Citation III followed a charter plane from Palermo when landing at Visp. The two planes parked side by side on the tarmac outside the small terminal building. The Italian passenger, in his black suit, black shirt, and white tie, looked a lot like Victor Mature in "Kiss of Death." The two Americans from the Citation, even in their Coogie sweaters, looked like anything but skiers here for the weekend. The Italian took a seat in the terminal to wait for someone. The Americans got into a waiting taxi to take them to the station in Visp. The pilots of the two aircraft were discussing the cross winds at this mountain valley airport.

At that same moment, a van with the group from Iraq was passing through St. Niklaus on their way to the car park in Tasch.

Kermit Blackmann and Ned O'Brien didn't have long to wait for the train. It was nearly full with skiers who had started the trip in Brig. They were lucky to find two seats together.

Later, while the train was stopped at the station at Randa to take on even more skiers, two cars passed on their way up to Tasch. One contained Tony Ruffini, along with Vittorio Mancini, the driver who picked him up at the airport shortly after the Americans left. The other car was being driven by Ridley Taylor from Bern.

When the two cars parked in the huge lot, near a police helicopter, in Tasch, they joined the throng of skiers waiting for the next train up the grade to Zermatt. Taylor made the Iraq team. He recognized General Hanfi from intelligence photos. He knew the woman must be the deadly Seraph Najim. He wasn't certain about the Italian twosome that looked like Victor Mature and his servant.

When the train arrived they all squeezed on board, taking every bit of available standing space. Ridley tried to stand near the Iraqis to see if he could overhear their conversation, but they stayed silent. Then he saw the Italian in the dark suit nod to the two Americans in new Coogie sweaters. The Denver Mining boys, Ridley thought. Maybe they hired some Italian muscle. My best move might be to contact the police. I could find out what's going on as an official from the American Embassy in Bern.

When the train unloaded in Zermatt, in addition to the multitude of skiers, four new entries were there to join Willi and Rudi in the hunt for the Keenes. Depending on who found them first, their lives were at risk.

Chapter 9

Wednesday, February 20
Day 3, Zermatt

Oblivious to all that was swirling around them, Clark and Lyn arose to the smell of bacon and coffee.

"A full skiers breakfast," Fran greeted them. She was never a health food nut. "It's such a beautiful day, maybe we can get some time in on the slopes."

"I don't know. Lyn and I need to think through these options. We need clothes. And we need to hear what Beaver has to say about the notebook."

"Where is Beaver?" Lyn asked.

"I sent him to the store to get you some toiletries and some fresh bread. You can wear some of our clothes."

Beaver came in a few minutes later, loaded with groceries, toiletries, and new ski suits for each of us. "I stayed up most of the night with your notebook. A lot of it I couldn't follow, as it was written in high German. And all the formulas and chemical compounds, I know nothing about. But it is about experiments to make gold from other metals. It appears no one has succeeded, but the author thinks that by putting together parts of the different experiments, it might work. I can tell you one thing, I'm fairly certain that this list of yours is not "The List." The writer keeps referring to a final list of Faust from the 1500's that has never been found. I think that is the list everyone is after."

"So we are being chased and threatened for something we don't even have," Lyn snapped.

"How about that," Clark added, "That dictates our option, though. I'm calling the major again. I'll tell him what we found is unimportant and that we are turning it over to the police in Zermatt. Then we can still make our flight tomorrow from Zurich to Boston."

"I agree, Dear. Let's call him after breakfast and put this behind us. Then, Fran, maybe we can go skiing for a while before we take the afternoon train back to Zurich."

It was a little after 9:00 when I called Willi's office in Zurich. "Major Wallis's office," a male voice answered in German.

"English?" I queried.

"Yes," the voice answered, "I am the major's deputy, Ulrich Hurd."

"I need to speak only to the major," I said, "My name is Keene, and I think the major is looking for me."

"He is, but he is not here. Please give me your phone number and I will have him call you back later."

"No, I would rather call back later myself."

"But he is out of the city. Your number, please."

"No. I'll call back at 10:30, one hour from now. You fix it so I can be transferred to the major at that time."

"Yes, I will set it up, Mr. Keene."

I hung up hoping I hadn't given time to have the call traced.

After he hung up, Officer Hurd contacted the phone company to see if they could tell where the call originated.

"No," the operator replied, "It was direct dialed."

"Okay." Hurd then called the equipment room to have a phone trap put on the major's line before the next call. After that he called Willi at police headquarters in Zermatt to set up the call. Willi was happy we were again trying to make contact.

At 10:00 that morning the train from Brig arrived with it's load of day skiers, eager to get to the lifts. The Iraq team started up the street, then stopped at the McDonalds for burgers and fries. They took a table by the window and began to discuss how to go about finding the Americans.

The Italians were more cautious, looking up the side streets and into each hotel and cafe. Vittorio told Tony, "I think I saw Jens Baer back there in the park across from the police station. He used to be the Zurich leader of the so called Aryan Elite.

"That's good, Vito. You take a place on that hotel terrace and watch him. I will continue our search up the street."

As Tony passed the McDonalds in the next block, Seraph Najim, seeing him, said, "That man was on our train. I have a bad feeling about him." She sent one of her assassins to follow him.

The two mining execs rode the electric cart up to the posh Mt. Cervin. It had rooms available because it was too expensive for the ski crowd. They asked the concierge to find them a knowledgeable local guide, one who knew the town and it's residents.

"That would be our retired police chief, Roland Eider. Let me call him. I will have him come here in just a few moments, as he lives just up there on the first plateau."

After a generous tip to the concierge, Kermit and Ned went into the restaurant to eat and wait for Eider. They were enthused about the possible pipeline this former chief might have into the police department.

When Chief Eider arrived, they filled him in on what they knew of the current situation. That both the police, as well as a number of unlawful groups, may be seeking some papers from an American couple. The couple may not even be aware of what is going on around them, although they have tried to contact the Zurich police.

"Our interests are strictly legitimate, Chief Eider," Kermit stated. "We simply want to buy the papers."

"Yes," added O'Brien, "They are very valuable to our businesses. They would be used for criminal purposes in the wrong hands."

"Why don't you just state your case to the police?"

"We have reason to believe that someone within the Zurich police may be working with the criminals," Kermit responded. "A detective from Zurich, a Major Wallis, is here leading the search."

"I've met him. He spoke at our national convention my last year as chief. He is a good man."

"Perhaps we are being over cautious, Chief," Ned replied, "But we would like for you to check it out discreetly for us. We're willing to pay as much as $10,000 for information."

Kermit quickly added, "We will pay $25,000 for the papers themselves."

"I'll check it out for you. Most of the Officers here were hired by me. I'll call you here when I have news."

"Thank you, Chief Eider." Ned and Kermit said in unison.

At that same time, Ridley Taylor was showing Major Wallis and Chief Mueller his diplomatic identity card. "I'm from the U.S. Embassy in Bern,"

he had said. "We have reason to believe that two of our citizens are the subject of a manhunt you're conducting."

"How did you come by that information Mr. Taylor? It is confidential police business." Willi asked.

"We have sources. In this case we were monitoring the satellite phone traffic of a terrorist group called the Aryan Elite and we taped a call from their Zurich leader, one Rudi Heiss, to Max Bormann in Berlin."

"Your information is very good and more than we had on that front," said Willi.

"Yes, Major, and I can offer more if we can work together. My interest is in the safety of our citizens."

Major Wallis filled him in, "We believe them to be innocently involved in all of this. They witnessed a murder in Zurich, probably committed by Rudi Heiss. Then they came into possession of a list that Heiss's organization wants. We have traced the Keenes here to Zermatt, where we believe they are staying with friends in a private home. We have officers out looking for them now, and I am awaiting a call from Mr. Keene at 10:30."

"You said their name was Keene. That we didn't have."

"We have their passport numbers, Mr. Taylor."

"Call me Ridley."

"I am Willi to everyone."

"Okay, Willi, give me those numbers and I'll have their files faxed here."

So everyone was either watching someone or checking with someone connected to the police search. All would be spurred into action by Clark's next call. If he had known that, he wouldn't have been as happy about the day's plans. He and Lyn were busy trying on their new ski suits, planning to spend a few hours on the slopes with their friends after handing over the notebook and list to the police.

Chapter 10

Wednesday, February 20
Day 3, Zermatt

We were all dressed for the slopes and had waxed the extra skis we left there on our earlier visit. I was getting ready to put in the call to Major Wallis, when Lyn reminded me, "Each time we call him, it seems the bad people are there. And isn't this call being patched through his Zurich office?"

"That's right, Honey, someone could listen in." I turned to Beaver and Fran, "Maybe we should call from a pay phone in the village."

"Don't be silly," Beaver said, "If you're concerned after the call, you and Lyn can ski out into the woods above the house. I'll answer the door when they come and you can come back in if it looks okay."

Lyn said, "We should take our things and the notebook just in case. You can tell them we got nervous and left, but you don't know where we went."

"Sounds good," Fran replied.

Lynn put our travel bag and new toiletries in a backpack while I dialed the phone. Willi's phone was answered on the first ring. This time in English. Ulrich assumed it was me, as it was exactly 10:30.

"I'll patch you through right away. The major is waiting for your call."

A few seconds later Major Wallis was on the line. "I am in Zermatt," he said, "and we think you are here, too. You were seen by a police officer boarding the train yesterday in Brig. So I came, hoping you would call."

"We came to stay with good friends, Frank and Fran Schultz."

"That would be Beaver," Willi smiled as he asked. "We have found out that much."

"I see. Yes, 'Beaver' is what we call him. The most important thing, though, is that this list and notebook are not 'The List' everyone is looking for."

"How do you know that?" Willi asked, somewhat surprised

"Beaver reads German. He says this is written in high German, and the notebook keeps referring to a list of a Dr. Faust who lived in the 16th century. I called to tell you we want out of this and that we would leave the book and list with the police here in Zermatt."

"You better stay where you are, Mr. Keene. Let us come to you. I suspect there is a leak in my office, so there may be others here looking for you."

"They seem to always be there first, Major."

"Yes, well I'm working on that problem. I want to finish this quick. There is also a representative of the U.S. Embassy here with me. He can help you get safely out of Switzerland."

"That sounds good Major, uh, Willi. It's the last lane on the left after you pass the cable car to Rifflealp. We are in the third chalet up the Gornergrat."

"We'll be there in ten minutes."

"He knows he has a mole in his office," Clark relayed excitedly. "And there is a man with him from the U.S. Embassy who wants to help. So, everything should be all right."

"I still think we should wait in the woods, Clark."

"You're right, Lyn," chimed in Fran. "Here's your back pack that has all your things, including the clothes you came in."

"Thanks!" we said together. Then we skied into the woods above the house, away from the town and closer to the cable way.

Minutes later we could see the police, four of them, Willi, and a taller man that we assumed was from the embassy coming up the street toward the lifts. As they turned up Beaver's path, we saw two other groups . . . a group of the Germans closely following the police . . . and the other an Arab looking team of four or five that moved like soldiers through the edge of the woods. Then, a moment later, two more toughs dressed in black came around the corner following the Germans. We wanted to warn Fran and Beaver, but had no way to do it.

When the police reached Beaver's steps, all hell broke loose. A shot rang out from the woods felling one of the policemen. The others dove for cover among the stilts on which the chalet was built. They took up defensive positions behind the poles. Then return fire came from down the slope, putting the chalet in the middle of a crossfire. A single shot rang out from further down the hill and one of the Germans screamed in mortal pain. People from all directions began firing at the chalet and at each other.

"We've got to get out of here, Lyn, head for the cable way."

"I sure hope Fran and Beaver are okay. Look what we have caused. The police will protect them, right Clark?"

"Well they are under their house, so I hope so." Shots were still ringing out when we reached the cable car. The sign said the pass to Italy was closed. That, combined with the sounds of the shooting, had all of the skiers out on the street. They were trying to find out what was going on. This allowed us to get on the next car.

As we rose from the valley floor, the shots became more distant. But not our fear for our friends. What had we done to them? At Rifflealp, we changed to the car to Furgg, and there we took the chair lift to Theodulhorn.

The operator at the top said in a mix of Italian and German, "Haven't seen many up this high today. The run over the top is closed. The snow hasn't been groomed. The run back down to Furgg is in good shape."

"Thanks," I replied, "We are expert skiers, but we won't do anything stupid. We may just go up a little way to get some pictures of the peaks. Then we'll ski back down to Furgg." I didn't tell him we didn't have a camera.

"Ja," he finished,

"Danke and Grazie," we said as we skied up the hill.

Back at the bottom the shooting had stopped. Beaver had kept yelling, "They're not here!" There were three dead: Officer Rolf Bartz of the local police, Jens Baer, who was Rudi's predecessor as leader of the Elite in Zurich, and Salim Zagara of the Iraq assassination squad. The wounded included Chief Mueller, who was shot in the leg, General Hanfi, who had a flesh wound to the torso, and Vittorio Mancini, who had sprained his ankle falling over the root of a pine tree. The different groups all retreated back down the hill. After a few minutes the major asked the remaining Zermatt officer, Walther Stout, to get an ambulance for Bruno and then to look for additional bodies or other evidence from the shooting. Then Willi and Ridley Taylor went inside.

"Where are the Keenes?" asked Willi.

"We were all concerned that you would be followed so they waited in the woods up above to see if it was safe," started Beaver.

"We were right, too!" added Fran, "Just look at this place."

"We'll compensate you for the repairs. Right now we need to focus on finding the Keenes."

"They were on skis. We were to signal if everything was all right and they were to come in. But I don't know what they would have done when the shooting started."

"Give the signal now, just in case."

Beaver went out on the balcony and waved his handkerchief over his head. Nobody came.

"They are both expert skiers and they know all the runs in the area, so they could be anywhere."

"We'll find them," Willi promised. "We have radioed the rescue team to finish up here. For your protection, I want you to go with us to headquarters. We can try to sort this out there."

The electric ambulance arrived as they were starting down the path. It passed them again down the street with Chief Bruno in the back giving them a thumbs up.

At the infirmary, the medical team determined the bullet had broken Bruno's femur in his left leg. They mended lots of broken legs, so he was in good hands.

Walther had found the two other corpses and sadly followed the body of his squad member, Rolf, down into town. The other two bodies were piled in the back of a luggage cart borrowed from a hotel.

When Major Wallis and Ridley Taylor saw them, Willi said, "This one is Jens Baer, former leader of the Aryan Elite in Zurich."

"And this one," Ridley said, "is, no doubt, one of the assassins from Iraq."

"You need to tell me about that, Ridley."

"Yes, Willi." It's funny how close you become to someone with whom you have shared a shoot out.

When they arrived at the police station, they left the Schultzes in the squad room and went in the back. "In addition to your German foes, Willi, we know Saddam Hussein has sent a team to recover the list. The are also two mining company executives here from Denver and a couple of tough looking Italian guys who, I think, are working for the mining guys."

"Why didn't you tell me all this? I should have had an army."

"You were in a hurry."

"Well, if we are going to work together, then we must share everything."

"I agree. I sure would like to talk to those two from Colorado."

As Willi and Ridley returned to the squad room, we had reached the top of the mountain and were looking down into Brueil-Cervinia on the Italian side of the Materhorn . . . Mt. Cervinia to them. "It hasn't been too bad so far, Clark. I think we can make it down."

"Okay, Honey, let's go for it! It's sure better than being shot at again."

Chapter 11

As we were working our way down to where the runs had been groomed, it was not very smooth going for our friends. They explained to the police that we had taken the notebook and the list. Beaver told them that while he had difficulty reading the high German, he felt certain that the real list everyone was looking for was one almost 500 years old. "The list the Keenes have is of names of people still alive."

"Who is on this current list?" the major asked.

Fran, with a little help from Beaver, came up with a priest in Rome named Corso, a professor, no name, in Heidelberg, someone named Gaspar in Palermo, and the places of Corfu and Staufen. "Oh," said Fran, "there also was a funny name from the U.S., like Kermit the frog."

"That was in the notebook," Beaver added, "It was with the names of some mining companies."

"Well, that's a good start. Please let me know if you remember more. What else about the notebook, Mr. Schultz?"

"It had to do with making gold. It discussed a number of failed attempts throughout history. I got the feeling that the writer thought by combining some parts of the different experiments, he or she might make it work."

"I'm no chemist," said Ridley, "but that's impossible."

"Some people don't agree, Rid. That's why we have all these players in this case," countered Willi.

"Now, what is your guess as to where your friends have gone?"

"They wanted out of this. They were scheduled to fly back to Boston from Zurich on Thursday. But after the shooting, I'd guess they went on with looking for the people on the list."

"I agree," said Fran, "They thought by finding out what the people on the list knew, they would be in a better position to bargain with you and the others."

"Foolish," muttered Willi.

"They are both expert skiers and know all the runs around here," Beaver began again. "They may have even gone across the top to Italy."

"The pass is closed," Jan, the leader of the ski squad, interjected. They had all come in when they heard the shooting. "I'll check with ol' Nick up at the top. He can tell us if he's seen them."

"Good," Willi was saying as she went into the other room to radio the station at Theodulhorn. The major asked two of the other Officers to escort Mr. and Mrs. Schultz back to their place and to stay there on guard. "They will be worried about you and may call. I want you tell them we want to help. I know they are worried about my office giving information to others. I am working on that. They could just tell you a meeting time and place and I will check with you periodically."

After Willi had sent them away, he called his superior in Zurich. "I want Ulrich Hurd from my staff picked up and held incommunicado until I return."

"What is this about, Major?"

"I'll explain fully when I return to Zurich. He may be providing police information to others."

"When will you be here?"

"Probably late this evening."

"I heard all the shooting," the former chief said as he entered the headquarters building. "What is going on?"

"This is our retired chief, Roland Eider. Roland, this is Major Wallis from the Zurich police."

"We've met," said Willi.

"Yes, Major, at the national conference a few years ago."

"Ah yes. Call me Willi. I never forget anyone as devoted to police work as you are."

"I've been retired two years now. Where is Bruno?"

"He was shot in the leg. Broken femur. They are fixing it now at the infirmary."

"Too bad. Any of our other men?"

"Yes Chief," said Walther, "Rolf was killed."

"My God, we have never lost a man except to ski accidents."

"We could use some help right now, Chief Eider," Willi interjected. "At least until Bruno is back on his feet."

"Okay, I'll be happy to help. But, first, let me tell you about a meeting I had this morning with two American businessmen."

"I'm Ridley Taylor, Chief, I'm from the U.S. Embassy. Were these two men wearing new Coogie sweaters?"

"They had on new sweaters, yes. They said they represented two mining companies from Colorado. They claimed their interests were legitimate. That they wanted to buy a list. They thought two other Americans here in Zermatt had this list and they wanted to hire me to find them."

"It is true. An American couple named Keene has a list that a number of people want," answered the major.

"I asked them why they just didn't go to the police. They knew you were after this couple and suggested that you might have an informant in your office."

"It seems everyone but me knew that. I think I have just plugged the leak."

"Anyway, they offered a huge sum—$10,000—to locate the Keenes, and $25,000 for the list itself."

"We still want your help, Roland. I know you'll do the right thing. It was this list that precipitated the shooting. We've learned that this list everyone is after may be worthless and that there is another old list which is the valuable one. That list disappeared 500 years ago, so this whole affair is lunacy."

"What do you want me to do, Willi?"

"I'd like to go with you, Chief, to meet with these businessmen," said Ridley. "Maybe we can convince them that they are wasting their time and send them back to Colorado."

"Okay with you, Roland?" Willi asked.

"Sure, Willi. I knew that money offer was too good to be true anyway."

As they were getting ready to leave, Jan came back in the room. "Chief Eider, good to see you."

"Hello Jan, you doing okay?"

"Yes sir. May I talk, Major?"

"Yes, the chief is going to work with us."

"Good. I talked with the operator at the top of the lift in Theodulhorn. He said two Americans got off the lift over an hour ago. He told them the pass was closed and that they should ski back down to Furgg. They told him they would be careful and that they only wanted to take some pictures before going back down. He hasn't seen them since."

"I have my helicopter standing by at Tasch. Can I go after them?" asked Willi.

"They're probably in Italy by now so you would have to get clearance from the Italian Air Ministry," she said.

"And that can take hours." added Roland. "Also, as the day goes on, the mountain makes it's own weather. It will be getting cloudy up there."

"We can call our friends at the station in Cervinia to watch for them," one of the other ski patrol officers suggested.

"Yes, do that," said Willi. "Rid, you and Roland go have your talk with the mining people and then report back here. I'll wait here to see what develops."

✣ ✣ ✣ ✣ ✣ ✣

Beaver and Fran were back in their chalet, surveying all the damage from the gun battle. Windows were shot out. Most of the good china in the hutch was broken. Even some of the wood furniture was in shreds.

"We are lucky we weren't hit," Fran sighed.

"Yeah, it sure didn't end like we thought. I hope Clark and Lyn are all right."

"Me too. I'll bet they headed to Cervinia."

"You're probably right, Fran. They'll call as soon as they can."

"Cervinia, ja!" one of two men entering the room from the kitchen said. Both had guns in their hands.

"Help!" Fran screamed.

"That will do you no good," the smaller of the two said as he pushed Beaver into a chair.

"Your two bodyguards have felt the knife of Rudi Heiss. You two will feel it also, unless you tell me all you know."

They were strong at first. They refused to answer any of the German's questions. Even as the larger one, Heinz, was beating Beaver and breaking his fingers, one by one.

But when Rudi told Heinz to start on Fran, Beaver said "No more, we will tell you what we know." They told them that the Keenes were on skis and had probably seen the shooting. That, even though the pass was closed, that they could have skied to Cervinia. Beaver told of his reading of the notebook which was about failed attempts to make gold. That "The List" that everyone was so excited about was not the one that their friends had. The real list had been lost 500 years ago in Staufen, Germany. He also told them they had told all of this to the police.

"What names were on this current list?" barked Rudi.

"A priest named Corso in Rome, a teacher at Heidelberg named Snell, or something like that, the Denver Mining Company in the U.S., and the towns Staufen, Corfu, and Palermo." After more torture, Fran remembered the name Gaspar went with Palermo.

Convinced he had all they knew, Rudi pulled out his stiletto and smiled as he efficiently killed them both.

"Now we have places to look Heinz. Let's go to Rome to see this priest."

Chapter 12

Wednesday, February 20
Day 3, Italy

We finally worked our way through the ungroomed snow down to where the runs were full of skiers. They come to Cervinia from Turin, Milan, and Aosta in Italy, as well as Chamonix and the Riviera in France. They come to ski in the daytime and to try their luck at the casino in St. Vincent at night.

It was easy going the rest of the way down to the village. We didn't want to spend much time there, as we assumed the police and our other pursuers would call ahead. We changed back into our other clothes in the ski house. After stuffing our ski gear into a rental locker and putting Beaver and Fran's skis in the check room under their name, we walked to the bottom of the hill where the bus departs for the train station in St. Vincent, at the base of the mountain in the Aosta Valley.

The next bus was leaving at 3:30 for the forty-minute ride down the twisting mountain road. We had only about twenty minutes to wait in the small bus stop enclosure. The only policeman we saw during our wait was one directing the constant stream of traffic in and out of the parking area across the road from the bus stop. We felt good about getting through Cervinia without incident.

When we arrived at the station in Challon-Saint Vincent, (it served both towns) we checked the winter schedules posted on the wall. There was a train leaving for Turin at 6:02 P.M., arriving there at the Porto Nova station at 7:35 P.M. We would have to wait there until 11:00 P.M. to catch the overnight train to Rome.

"Should we reserve a sleeper, Clark?"

"No, we would have to give our name. Let's just use our Eurrail passes. We can take our chances on the train."

The train arrived in Turin on time. Rather than wait around the station for three hours, with the chance of being seen, we decided to go out and find a place for dinner. We realized we had had nothing to eat since Fran's big breakfast that morning. With that thought, all of a sudden we were starving.

We walked down the Via Roma, Turin's main shopping street, and stopped in a department store. We thought we needed to change our appearance to have a better chance of reaching Rome. We both bought new hats, sunglasses, and jackets. Lyn bought a scarf and I got an inexpensive briefcase to replace the backpack.

Then we turned off the Via Roma on to Via Andrea Doria where we found the Balbo restaurant. It is an attractive two story spot with an excellent menu. Lyn ordered the tortolloni stuffed with asparagus. I had branzino, bass marinated in basil. Once we settled down, I said, "I sure hope Fran and Beaver are okay."

"Me too, Clark. Can we call them?"

"Not yet, Honey. Let's wait a day or two in case their phone is tapped."

"We should at least write and tell them where we left their skis. We could send the key for our ski clothes, too."

"Okay, we'll write them on the train. What do you think we should do when we get to Rome?" I asked.

"Well, Clark, if I were going to make a list of options like you do, I would say we could:"

Call Willi again

Find this Monsignor Corso to see what he knows

Contact the U.S. Embassy.

"I vote for finding Monsignor Corso, and then contacting the U.S. Embassy," I replied, "This priest must be important or he wouldn't be on the list."

"Right. Do you think the police or any of the others know where we are, or where we're going?"

"Not unless Beaver shared the list with them. He may have with the police, trying to help us."

"That could be, Clark. He or Fran may have shared it with them to show it isn't 'The List.' They would think that might stop the chase, if Major Wallis's snitch passed it on."

"It may, or may not. If they are like us, they may think this list will lead them to the other."

We sat at the restaurant over cappuccinos until 10:30. Then we returned to the station. Since our overnight train originated in Turin, it was already on the track. We boarded the first class car and scanned the reservation slips on each compartment until we found one that wasn't reserved. We had changed our Swiss currency to Italian lire at the station and bought books, magazines, and snack items. We spread these on the other seats to discourage other passengers from joining us, figuring that most of the people who would travel first class probably would book sleeping compartments on a nine hour, overnight journey.

We were wrong. As the departure time drew near, we were joined by a family of four. A young Italian couple with two small children. It was going to be a long night. Then, after departure, when the conductor came to check the tickets, I asked him if there were any available sleeping compartments.

"Si, Signore, we have had a cancellation." For a small fee, in addition to the cash we paid to upgrade, we were moved to the sleeping car and our own room.

We talked more as we waited for sleep. The events of the day were burned into our memories. We continued to worry about the Schultzes. We reaffirmed our plan to try to find the priest first and then contact our embassy. We decided we would try to get a room at the Hotel Senato, a place where we were known from our four previous visits to the Eternal City.

I had a strange feeling that we would see the same cast of characters in Rome that had been in Zermatt. Then sheer exhaustion took over and sleep came.

Chapter 13

While we had been working our way across the Materhorn and down into Italy, the other parties were back in Zermatt deciding on their next move.

Rudi Heiss and Heinz Ruppert made a hasty trip down the service road to Tasch after their torturing and murdering of Fran and Beaver. They retrieved their car and started the drive to Visp.

✤ ✤ ✤ ✤ ✤ ✤

The Iraqi team had left an hour earlier on the train, retrieved their van in Tasch, and were already in Brig. There, General Hanfi and Seraph Najim agreed they should separate. Yousef was to drive the general back to Zurich where he could find out from the police mole, Ulrich, where the Americans had gone. Then the general would return to Baghdad to report to Saddam Hussein and to receive medical treatment, beyond the bandage they had applied, for his flesh wound. Seraph and her remaining assassin, Abdul Kareem, would wait at the bottom of the road from Zermatt to try to pick up the trail.

✤ ✤ ✤ ✤ ✤ ✤

The Italians, with Vittorio limping badly, were on the next train. They decided to abandon their car at Tasch and ride the train to Visp. There Tony boarded the waiting charter plane and was over the Mediterranean on his way back to Palermo. Vittorio was to take the train back to Zurich.

✢ ✢ ✢ ✢ ✢ ✢

The Americans from Homestead Mines and Denver Mining were still at the Mt. Cervin. They had visited with Chief Eider and the embassy man, Ridley Taylor. They were waiting for their respective offices to open in Denver, at 4:00 Zermatt time, so they could discuss whether to continue looking for this wrong list.

✢ ✢ ✢ ✢ ✢ ✢

The police were busy. Ridley Taylor received a faxed copy of the Keene's passport files with pictures. Major Wallis circulated the pictures through Interpol to all European police agencies. Ridley also alerted the other U. S. Embassies, with a particular note to Rome that the couple may be heading there.

It was only after Willi sent Officer Walther Brandt up to check on the Schultz couple and their two police guards that roadblocks were set up on the road to Visp and at the train stops along the way. Walther had radioed back the alarm as soon as he saw his two dead comrades outside the chalet. Then he became ill when he saw the carnage inside. The major, Ridley, and former Chief Eider all went to the scene.

"What do you make of it, Rid?" Willi asked.

"Looks like some of the bad guys must have come back to find out what these two knew."

"I agree," said Eider. "From the looks of it, they held out for quite a while." Willi had been looking over the bodies. "The final blow was a knife. A small blade. I'd say by Rudi Heiss. The stiletto is his favorite weapon. That's what killed the victim in the Baur au Lac night before last."

"We must assume they now know everything we know, Major. I need to call my embassy so they'll alert the Keenes if they do call."

"First, Walther, call all the police on the way down the mountain to set up roadblocks and to check all the trains coming down. I'm going to take my copter down to Visp to refuel, and then go back to Zurich. I want to interrogate Hurd. Then I plan to fly to Rome. My bet is they're headed there to find this Monsignor Corso."

"I'll drive back to Bern. Then I plan to go to Rome. I'll be at our embassy there with Ken Merrill, if you want to reach me," Ridley said.

"Good." Willi replied. "They may try to contact your people. I assume they probably witnessed the shoot-out. They may recognize you as one of the good guys." Then he looked at the retired chief and asked, "Chief Eider, I would appreciate it if you would take charge here until Chief Mueller is able to take over."

"I would be happy to help out, Major."

"Good, here is my private number. They can always reach me. Walther, can you drive Mr. Taylor and me down to Tasch."

"Sure, Willi, I'll get the Land Rover."

After they were gone and Chief Eider had overseen the removal of the bodies, he stopped by the Mt. Cervin to inform the two executives he had met that morning of the additional deaths. "I think there is nothing more for you here in Zermatt. Major Wallis of the Zurich police and your U.S. Embassy man, Mr. Taylor, have left."

"Where to?" asked Kermit casually.

"Rome," the old chief said before realizing he probably should not have told them. Age makes us all a little forgetful.

"Thank you, Chief. We understand why you couldn't fulfill our request from this morning. But we do feel we owe you a retainer, as it is our fault you are now involved. Please take this envelope with our thanks."

Ned added, "We will take your advice and leave the first thing tomorrow morning."

The chief waited until he was outside before opening the envelope. Two thousand U.S. dollars. For nothing. He hoped again he hadn't made a mistake by mentioning Rome.

After he was gone, it was time to contact Denver. But instead of discussing the next move, both Kermit and Ned reported they were on the trail and would be going to Rome. Kermit told his Secretary, Norma, to book the two of them into the Hassler in Rome and to contact the pilots and have them ready to fly to Rome by 9:00.

As Rudi and Heinz were approaching Randa, they could see the line of traffic stopped below them. They could see it was a road block. They pulled over in an emergency stopping area behind a camper. The camper had a flat and a young Austrian man was trying to change the tire.

"Can we help?" Rudi said with a smile.

"Ja, Danke!"

While Heinz helped change the tire, Rudi checked out the trailer. A pretty blonde wife and a small baby . . . perfect, he thought. When the tire was replaced, Rudi pulled his knife and took the baby from it's mother. "We must get through that roadblock he told the couple. We will be with your wife and child in the trailer. You tell the authorities that they are the only ones here and they are sleeping. If they come to check," he said to the woman, "you can open the door and tell them it is all right."

The police at the Randa roadblock accepted the husbands story without checking. At St. Niklaus they did knock on the trailer door. They then believed the wife, and they were on the way to Visp. Just before entering the town, Rudi made them pull over. They detached the trailer. Rudi and Heinz drove off in the truck which had pulled the trailer, leaving the three bodies with clean knife wounds inside the trailer. They planned to drive to Milan's Linate Airport where they could get an Alitalia flight to Rome. They would have to stop in Brig to get false papers and cash from the cell there. They were always prepared for such things. Rudi knew he would have to report to Bormann.

At their cell house, Rudi placed the call to Max Bormann in Berlin. He described the shoot-out and the information he had elicited from the friends of the Keenes. He emphasized the fact that the list they had and the notebook were of little value, hoping Max would be more tolerant.

"You are right to go to Rome to find this priest and the Keenes. I am sending Rolf to join you. He will meet you at our house in Trastavere tomorrow." Rolf Strang was the only man in the Aryan Elite more ruthless and more skilled than Rudi. Rudi knew Max was sending him to take charge and to punish him if they were to fail. "I will not fail" he pledged to himself as he rejoined Heinz in the truck for the drive to Milan.

Seraph and Abdul had seen the two Germans detaching a trailer from a truck when they returned to the mountain road. They were now following the truck at a safe distance through the Simplon tunnel into Italy.

Chapter 14

We arrived in Rome at 7:50 the next morning, about forty minutes behind schedule. Both Lyn and I had slept soundly on the train. The tension of the previous day and the exertion of skiing across the top of the Materhorn had left us exhausted. The porter had awaken us just fifteen minutes before we reached Rome's Termini station.

"I feel good," I said as I was dressing.

"Me too, Dear, the sleep really helped. What should we do first?"

"Let's get breakfast at the station. Then we can take a taxi to the Senato and see if Georgio has a room for us. We can start our search for this Monsignor Corso from there."

"Good plan, Clark, I'm famished."

No one at the station seemed to be paying any attention to us. There were police patrolling the place, and we saw one black leather coated blonde man scanning the passengers from our train as we exited the platform. Our change of clothes, sunglasses, and briefcase enabled us to slip by without challenge. No one followed us into the restaurant. After eating some excellent hard rolls and salami, washed down by our usual tea and hot chocolate, we cashed some travelers checks at the bank in the station. Outside we got in the first taxi in line and gave directions to the Hotel Senato.

It's a smaller hotel on one side of the Piazza della Rotonda, the square on which the Pantheon sits. The Pantheon was built around A.D. 125 by Emperor Hadrian. It is the best preserved of all the ancient Roman structures and it has been continuously used through all the centuries. The Pantheon attracts a multitude of visitors, so the remainder of the square is cafes and bars with their tables spilling out into the piazza. We had stayed at the Senato on four previous visits to Rome. Not only for the view of the Pantheon from our room, but also because of the location between the Piazza Navonna on one side and the Roman Forum on the other. Plus, Lyn could walk to the shops in the Via Condotti district. But more than the central location, we liked the hotel because of the concierge, Georgio Ginasi. He knew everything about Rome and could arrange for whatever we decided was worth doing.

When we arrived at the Senato with only our travel shoulder bag, we were pleased to see that Georgio was on duty.

"Ah, Mr. and Mrs. Keene. We were not expecting you. Did we miss a reservation?"

"No, Georgio, this unplanned and very sudden. We were in Switzerland and, by accident, received something that now some German criminal types have been after. They were chasing us in Zermatt and we decided we would be safer in Italy."

"Plus," Lyn interjected, "there is a list they want, and there is the name of a priest here in Rome on that list. We want to find him."

"What is his name. The Vatican has a directory of all clergy worldwide. We can check with them."

"His name is Monsignor Corso."

"No need to check the directory. Here." Georgio reached under the counter and pulled out a tourist brochure on the Vatican Museum. On the back it listed the Curator as Monsignor Ricardo Corso, and it gave his phone number.

"But now let me find you a room. Your usual front corner room is occupied. I have a middle front on the third floor."

"That's fine. We had to leave in a hurry, Georgio, so we also are without clothes."

"No problem," he returned, his frequent answer, "Just make a list of what you need and I will have it filled. We can charge the things to your room."

"Thank you. There is one more thing you can help us with. Police officers may also be looking for us. We have done nothing wrong and they know that. But each time we try to contact the one in charge, these Germans show up. So we need to stay incognito if possible."

"No problem, we have three days before we are required to file your passport numbers with the police."

"That should be more than enough time, Georgio. Thank you again."

"Please, go up to your room, number 302. I will call Monsignor Corso to arrange an appointment. Would you like some . . . it's tea and hot chocolate, right."

"Yes, very good Georgio," Lyn said.

On the new elevator since our last visit, Lyn said "Isn't he amazing."

"You bet. He is the best."

We found our room, opened the drapes so we could look out on the piazza, and waited for Georgio to work his magic. Little did we know that all of our pursuers were on their way to Rome.

Chapter 15

Thursday, February 21
Day 4, Rome

Rome's Fumincino Airport was busy that morning. A Citation III was among the corporate aircraft arriving. This one from Visp in Switzerland. The Alitalia flights from Milan's Linate were always full. No one paid any attention to the two Germans that hastily made their way to the taxi line and asked to be taken to an address in the Trastavere section. That is, no one except the attractive dark-haired woman with the middle eastern features.

Seraph and Abdul had observed their quarry buying tickets at the Rome shuttle desk in Milan, so they did the same. She tried to stay close enough to hear their directions to the driver of the taxi, but she couldn't without being observed. She was able to get the number off the cab. That would be enough.

Blackmann and O'Brien took a prearranged limo to the Hassler where their rooms had been rented the night before so they could arrive early. On the way into town, Ned asked "What do you suggest we do next, Kerm?"

"I think we should call the embassy's business liaison and explain our problem to them. That Taylor was with the State Department, probably a C.I.A person. He may have been in contact with the embassy here.

"Good idea. Let's call them for an appointment. We could meet with the ambassador if necessary. We both know people at the White House who could set it up."

"Okay, I'll make the call."

Ridley Taylor had returned to Bern, reported in to Bryan Roberts on all of the details of the shoot-out, the murders, and the suspicion that the Keenes had gone to Rome to see this Monsignor Corso. "I'm booked to Rome on the late morning flight. Have Kenny Merrill meet me at Fumincino at 12:30 Rome time. I'm on Swissair, number 266."

"Okay, Rid, stay in touch. Cathy did catch another message from our friend Rudi in Brig to Bormann in Berlin. His description of the doings in Zermatt pretty much follows yours. He also said he and Heinz were going to Rome and would go to a safe house in Trastavere. I'll ask Kenny to locate it before you get there."

"Good, Bryan. Thanks!"

Anthony Ruffini had arrived back in Palermo the evening before. He was meeting with Gaspar and the don in Corleone. "There were more than two groups involved in the shooting, Sir. The police, and another group that was following them, and still another group hiding in the woods. I'm sure I got one of the Germans, Sir."

"It's all right, Tony, you didn't go in prepared for that. And Vittorio is not cut out for that kind of trouble."

"No. He fell over a tree. That was funny. At least it did keep him out of my way."

"We will wait until Vittorio hears from his informant. Then we will decide what to do."

"Good plan, Padrone," Gaspar and Tony said in unison.

"You pick a couple of the boys and get them ready for your next trip."

"Yes, Sir."

In Zurich, Major Wallis was questioning Ulrich Hurd. "I trusted you, Ulrich," he bellowed. "I promoted you to be my assistant and you betrayed me for money. It will be a long time before you will ever spend any of it, you jackal."

"I'm sorry sir. I should not have gotten myself involved with these people."

"I don't want to hear your excuses. Lock him up."

"But sir, I can be of value. I know the Aryan Elite organization. I pretended to be a part. I know they have a place in Rome. I have been there for a meeting."

"Where," Willi demanded, "Where?"

"I don't know the address. But I can take you there."

"Yes, you will, in irons. Wanda," he said to the girl taking notes, "arrange for two officers to be his escort and book the police Lear jet to take us all to Rome.

They arrived at Fumincino at 2 P.M. The stage was now set for another round.

Chapter 16

Thursday, February 21
Day 4, Rome

We both were asleep when Georgio called our room at 11:00 to tell us he had arranged an appointment with Monsignor Corso for 5:00 that afternoon. He was a marvel!

We made out our clothing shopping list and dropped it off at the desk on our way out to lunch. Not wanting to chance being seen in the city, we decided to have lunch at one of our all time favorite restaurants, the Cecillia Metella, which is out on the Appia Antica (the old Appian Way) across the road from the Catacomba San Sebastiano. The view from the terrace of the restaurant is of the tomb of Cecillia Metella, concubine to one of the Roman Emperors.

It was a sunny, mild day so we first walked over to the Piazza Navonna to look at the various artists' displays. We had two paintings purchased on previous trips in our home, and we always enjoyed browsing. After about an hour of walking amongst the stalls, we went out the south end of the Piazza and caught a taxi at the stand on Corso Vittorio Emanuelle II.

The restaurant had not set up the tables on the terrace, as the season for tourists had not yet begun. Inside there were a few tables occupied by business people, gesticulating their luncheon discussions. We were given a table by the window overlooking the terrace toward the tomb. Lyn, predictably, ordered their linguine alla vongole. She loved their white clam sauce. For a second course, she had their house special, scrieno, a delicate grape cannelloni. I liked everything they served and their large portions. Italian food is one of my weaknesses. As usual, I ordered two pasta courses.

I started with tortellini en brodo, followed by veal milanaise with bucatini ragu on the side. I ordered a nice bottle of Bolla Bardolino, what I jokingly call the Keene family ancestral wine, to wash it all down. You could almost forget your problems at a meal like that.

Lyn interrupted my gastronomic delight with, "What are we going to tell the Monsignor?"

"I think the best bet is to tell him the truth. How we came to get the notebook and the list with his name on it. The fact that we're the subjects of multiple manhunts. And then ask him why his name would be on the list."

"That's pretty much the same as I've been thinking, Clark. I want to ask him about Leonardo DaVinci, too."

"Yes, hopefully he will explain the reason for all the interest in this so called 'list'."

After a tiramasu for me and some chocolate gelato for Lyn, we asked the waiter to call a taxi. One was there in ten minutes. We told the driver to take us to the Vatican Museum, the employees entrance, which was the direction given to Georgio.

We arrived at 4:15 and decided to wait outside on a bench until closer to our 5:00 appointment. The crowd of visitors down the street at the main entrance was starting to thin, but even at this time of year there were numerous tour groups exiting the museum and boarding their buses. I entertained myself timing the span between when the first of the group would board the bus to the last. There was always at least one laggard anywhere from ten to twenty minutes late. At 4:50 we entered the museum and told the guard at the desk we had an appointment with Monsignor Corso.

"Yes, Mr. and Mrs. Keene, he is expecting you. I will have a guide take you up."

A young woman appeared from the next room and asked us to follow her. We took an elevator to the fifth level and entered a large workshop area where several people were laboring over paintings, statuary, and other artifacts being prepared for display in the museum. At the far end of the workshop we came to a set of offices. Monsignor Corso's was the last in the row, in a corner looking out over the Vatican's lovely gardens.

He rose to greet us. "I don't get so many visitors from America, Mr. and Mrs. Keene, please sit down and tell me how I can serve you."

He was a tall man with white hair and a well trimmed white beard and mustache. He could have passed as a Maine lobsterman. His smile and demeanor encouraged us to be forthright with him.

"We have an unusual tale to tell you, Monsignor, with regard to this list. You can see your name is there next to the letters 'DV'. But let me start at the beginning."

Lyn and I recounted the entire story of our becoming involved by chance and of finding the locker key, the notebook, and the list in the Zurich station. We told him of our being chased and of the shooting in Zermatt. Then of our escape over the Materhorn and trip here to see him. We also told him that our friends, the Schultzes, may have told the police that his name is on this list.

"If they did give your name to them, you may get several more visitors, Monsignor Corso."

"May I see the notebook?" he asked.

"Certainly," said Lyn pulling it from our travel bag. He studied it for a few minutes.

"Very interesting," he said, "I read high German. This notebook is the work of a student preparing for a Doctoral thesis in chemistry. As a topic the student chose past experimentation in artificially making gold. I would like to study this in detail. I can tell you now, the reason I am on the list is because of my position as curator of this museum. You see, Leonardo DaVinci was one of the principal experimenters of this notion that gold could be made from base metals."

"When was that," Lyn asked.

"The early 1500s, Mrs. Keene. Pope Leo the Tenth was the leader of the church from 1513 to 1521. He was a part of the Medici family, he was constantly making war on someone and granting indulgences to those who would help finance his forays. He was having difficulty with a priest, Martin Luther, up in Wittenberg, Germany, over those indulgences. In a move to get the funds he needed, he hired Leonardo to continue his experiments in alchemy here at the Vatican. He lent the Cabinet of the Apoxyomenos rooms to DaVinci for three years. From what we know today, DaVinci set up an elaborate apparatus to try and change the basic structure of lead through an ionization process and by adding other compounds into gold. It seems Leonardo learned it couldn't be done. But he liked living here at the Vatican under the sponsorship of the Pope. He began using the rooms for some of his other drawings. After three years, the Pope evicted DaVinci when he learned he was using the rooms to study ladies of easy virtue for his gynecological drawings."

"What became of his experiment notes and his apparatus?" I asked.

"We still have them somewhere in storage, I'm sure. We never throw anything away."

"Thank you, Monsignor, that is very helpful," said Lyn.

"If you will leave the notebook with me, I will read the rest and perhaps I can tell you about the others on the list."

I replied, "We would really appreciate that, Sir. But we've found we need to be ready to run at any moment. Is it possible for you to make a copy of the book and list, so we can keep the original."

"Certainly," he said as he pushed a button on his desk. A young priest entered the office and, at the Monsignor's instructions, took the notebook and list to make a copy.

While he was gone, I said, "You may hear from a Major Wallis of the Zurich police. We think he is trying to help us, but he has someone in his office who is feeding information to the other people after us. If he does contact you, please tell him we want to cooperate as soon as we know it's safe."

"I'll tell him."

"We also plan to go to the U.S. Embassy here in Rome," Lynn added, "There was an embassy man with the police in Zermatt."

The young priest returned with the copies. Monsignor Corso handed us the originals and said, "I will call you at the Senato tomorrow to let you know about the rest of the names."

"Oh, oh," said Lyn, "Please don't tell anyone where we are staying."

"I won't. We priests are very good at keeping secrets."

"Until tomorrow then," I said as I rose from my chair.

"Yes, until tomorrow. Your guide is waiting outside to show you out. And I will call the guard to have a taxi waiting for you. It gets very busy around here at this time of day."

As we left the building and entered our waiting cab, Lyn said, "I like him."

"Me too, Honey. Let's hope we haven't gotten him in any trouble."

"I'm still worried about Beaver and Fran," she said.

"Me too."

Chapter 17

Thursday, February 21
Day 4, Rome

While we were spending the day dining at one of our favorite restaurants and meeting with the Monsignor, the other players were also busy.

Ridley Taylor had been met by Ken Merrill and driven to the embassy on the Via Veneto. They went to brief the ambassador, Robert Law, on the situation. As they entered his office he said, "I've already had an alert on your situation from Washington. The president is meeting with your director and certain other advisors at 4:00 our time, about three hours from now. They ask that we do nothing until then."

"Okay, Sir. I do think we should tell the front gate and reception that if the Keenes show up, to send them to my office," Ken requested.

"Yes, I'll take care of that. I'll call you when I hear from Washington again."

They went to Merrill's office where Ridley called Bryan Roberts. "I know it's hard to find me sometimes, but what the hell is going on. I hear the president is now in on this op."

"Right, Rid. We've been waiting for you to call. When Bush heard that Iraq was involved, he invited everyone, State, Defense, Treasury, the Joint Chief, and others to a meeting at 10:00. Director Webster is to make the presentation. Cathy, Brendan, and I met with the director and gave him your report on the shootings and murders in Zermatt. After looking at all the options, we're going to recommend to the President that we leave the Keene couple out in the cold as bird dogs for you."

"That's crazy. They don't have any idea what they are involved in and they have no training in these matters."

"They've done pretty well so far."

"Blind luck, Bryan."

"Advance thinking, Rid."

"Maybe."

"We just think that you and Ken can protect them and wipe up some of these bad guys at the same time."

"Do you think the President will go for it?"

"I think he will be willing to use them if it has a chance to foil Saddam."

"Let us know when we get our marching orders." After he hung up, Ridley briefed Ken and then said, "Let's get some good Italian food."

"You're in the right country, Rid."

The ambassador had received the request for a meeting with the two mining executives. He stalled it until Friday morning. He had his secretary tell them he was out of the city today. He wanted the results of President Bush's meeting first. Thus, Kermit Blackmann and Ned O'Brien started thinking about where they might dine that night.

Major Wallis, along with his Italian chaperones, Ulrich, and his guards arrived at Piazza Santa Maria della Scala in Trastevere. They left their cars there and walked to a building on Via Mattonato behind the church. Two of the Italian police went around to the alley to cover the back. Ulrich was being watched by the two Swiss officers in an alcove across the street. Willi and the remaining two Italians went to the door and knocked.

"Who is it?"

"Polizia," cried the Italian lieutenant. They could hear scrambling within the house. The lieutenant shot off the lock and the three of them charged in. Then they heard an exchange of shots from the alley. They ran out to find two Germans down, one dead and one dying. The two Italian police were also dead. One by gunshot and one by stiletto. They called for help and had Ulrich brought around.

"The dead one is Heinz Ruppert. He was with Rudi in Zurich and in Zermatt. The wounded one is the local Aryan leader in Rome. I don't know his name," said Ulrich of the unconscious man with a wound to the head.

A search of the house revealed considerable armor: Uzis, a variety of pistols, sniper rifles, shotguns, knives, and a room full of plastique explosives and bomb making equipment. While sorry about the loss of his men, the lieutenant was pleased with the capture of this arsenal. Major Wallis was sorry that Rudi and one other had gotten away. They found three passports in a bedroom. While they carried Polish names, one picture was of Rudi, one of Heinz, and one Willi didn't recognize. He showed it to Ulrich who cringed when he saw it.

"That is Rolf Strang. He is Max Bormann's muscle from Berlin. A very dangerous man."

More police officers and the medical team had arrived. After telling the inspector in charge what had happened, Major Wallis asked the lieutenant to take him to the jail where they could lock up Ulrich. Then he called his office in Zurich and told the chief about the additional killings.

"No calls from your American couple. A Mr. Taylor from the U.S. Embassy called to say he is at their embassy in Rome. He is with a Ken Merrill."

"Thank you, Chief. I'll call again tomorrow." Then Willi called the U.S. Embassy and asked for Mr. Merrill.

"Merrill here."

"This is Major Wallis of the Zurich police. Is Ridley Taylor with you?"

"Right here, Major."

Ridley came on the line. "Willi, that you? Been in any more shoot-outs?"

"As a matter of fact, yes. Here in Rome about two hours ago."

"Were the Keenes involved?"

"No, I had found the leak in my office. He led us to the Aryan Elite safe house here in Rome."

"You okay?"

"Yes, but two Italian policemen and two of the Aryans are down."

"Wow. We need to talk, Willi. I have information from my government. I should say I'll have official directions sometime around five or six. Can you meet us for dinner."

"Yes, I have no plans."

"Good. We'll meet you at 8:00 tonight at Da Bolognese. It's on the Piazza del Popolo."

"See you at 8:00," Willi said as he hung up the phone. The plot thickens, he thought.

Chapter 18

Thursday, February 21
Day 4, Washington

Seated around the table in the president's private conference room off of the oval office were Secretary of State James Baker, Secretary of the Treasury Nicholas Brady, Secretary of Defense Dick Cheney, Chairman of the Joint Chiefs Colin Powell, and the Director of the Central Intelligence Agency William Webster.

When President Bush entered the room, they all started to rise. "Stay seated, please. All right, Bill, bring us all up to speed."

The director of the CIA began, "We have a potentially bad situation developing in Europe. Two of our citizens, unofficial tourists, came into possession of certain materials in Zurich that, purportedly, describe a method for manufacturing gold. While our experts tell us this cannot be done, there are a number of groups who think it can. In addition to the Swiss police who are trying to find this couple—their name is Keene and you have copies of their passport files in your folder —there is a neo-nazi group called the Aryan Elite, the Mafia, a consortium of U.S. mining companies, and the reason for this meeting, the Iraq Secret Service after them."

"How about your people?" asked the president.

"We have our number one operative, Ridley Taylor, on the case, Sir. And we have alerted all our European stations. But let me continue. Taylor reported a shoot-out in Zermatt, where the Keenes had gone to hole up with friends. The Keenes escaped and are believed to be in Rome. Taylor and the police learned from the Keene's friends that this list included a priest named Corso, in Rome.

"Shortly after that, these friends, U. S. citizens from Illinois, Frank and Fran Schultz, were tortured and murdered along with their two Swiss police guards. Taylor is already in Rome where he and our station chief there, Ken Merrill, will try to locate this priest and the Keenes. We are not certain about which of the others know what. We do know a charter aircraft returned from the airport at Visp, which is the closest to Zermatt, to Palermo. We assume that is the Mafia party. We also know that two executives from the mining group filed a flight plan for their corporate plane from Visp to Rome. Taylor had met with them in Zermatt and tried to dissuade them from acting on their own. They have a meeting scheduled with Ambassador Law tomorrow morning."

"What about the Iraqis?" asked Cheney.

"We're not certain. There were three fatalities during the shoot out. One was an Iraqi, Salim Zagara, who is a member of Seraph Najim's assassination squad. Also killed were one of the Zermatt police officers and Jens Baer, the former head of the Aryan Elite in Zurich. The rest of the Iraq team included General Hanfi, Saddam's chief of secret service, Najim, who I mentioned, and another of her assassins, Abdul Kareem. We got their names from an Emirates Air flight to Zurich the night before."

"Tell me more about this Nazi organization," queried Powell.

"It's the legacy of Martin Bormann, Hitler's chief of staff. His body was never located in the Berlin bunker. It's believed he escaped to South Africa or Brazil and later died. The Elite promotes the 'master race' theme of Hitler. The group has only had two leaders, Bormann's son Manfred and, after his death, the grandson, Max. They are a fairly large organization with members all over the world. They encourage and train the leaders of these 'skinhead' groups who continue to cause problems. They would be much worse if they had the necessary funds. We believe they have depleted the fortune Martin Bormann squirreled away in Swiss accounts. Hence, their interest in this business about making gold."

"I can't even estimate the problems we would face if such a thing were possible." Treasury Secretary Brady took the floor. "World financial markets would collapse. All those countries who owe us hundreds of billions of debt, their currency would become valueless. As would our stockpile of gold at Fort Knox. Our economy would also collapse. It would be a catastrophe of gigantic proportions."

"If Hussein had such a capability, Mr. President," added Secretary Cheney, "he could dictate the terms of our surrender."

"Then that must not happen, Dick. General, how close are you to starting the ground operation of Desert Storm?"

"We are nearly ready now, Sir. The weeks of bombing have obliterated their communication systems and we have complete control of their airspace."

"Give the order to General Schwarzkopf. We can't afford to delay."

"Yes Sir. We have been meeting with Norman over the last three days. He says it will take two days to have everyone in position. I'll inform you of the exact time."

"Webster, I want your man, Taylor, to find these Keenes and get whatever they have."

"May I suggest, Sir, that from what this Frank Schultz told us, what the Keene's have is not 'The List.' It is a list of people who may be able to assist in finding the real list. We think we should find, but then closely follow, the Keenes. We can protect them, apprehend the other groups involved, and then pick them up if they actually find the true list."

"I agree," chimed in the treasury chief. "I cannot stress enough the importance of our having that list."

"If it really exists," added Secretary Baker.

"How about the rest of you? Cheney?"

"I agree."

"Powell?"

"Yes."

"Then it looks like we let two of our citizens volunteer for some national service. Keep me posted. I have to go speak to the V.F.W. convention. Too bad I can't tell them we are about to start the ground action in the Gulf."

Lyn and Clark Keene did not know they had just become the bait in a game of international intrigue.

Chapter 19

Thursday, February 21
Day 4, Rome

Ambassador Law got the call from the president himself at 5:30. "How are things in my favorite city, Bob? How's Judy?"

"Both fine, Mr. President. I wasn't expecting you to call."

"Just want to emphasize the importance of this operation. It seems this couple, Clark and Lyn Keene, live not too far from our place in Kennebunkport, seems they can perform an invaluable service for their country if they keep going on this hunt for this list. May even shorten the war. By the way, I have ordered Desert Storm ground operations to begin within the next few days. Anyway, those CIA fellows you have there, have them get hold of Bryan Roberts. He'll explain it all to them."

"I will, Mr. President. You can count on us."

"I do. You and Judy should come home sometime this summer. Barbara and I can take you up to Camp David for the weekend."

"We'd like that, Sir."

"Gotta go, Bob, I have a group of Boy Scouts waiting in the East Room. Then a D.A.R. convention speech at lunch."

"Yes Sir. Good-bye."

The ambassador told Ridley and Ken about the call from the president. They had it explained to them again when they reached Bryan Roberts. Then they exchanged that information with Willi, over dinner, for his update on the Aryan Elite.

"One strange thing was discovered on the autopsies of the bodies in Trastevere. The policeman was shot by Heinz Ruppert's gun. The local

Aryan was shot by one of the police. But the bullet that killed Ruppert was fired from a rifle," Willi said with a puzzled look on his face.

"Sounds like Seraph Najim and her team may have been in the war zone," mused Ridley.

"That's probably it," Willi agreed.

"Come to the embassy in the morning, Willi. Bring your Italian police host. We can discuss our next moves and how we can go about locating the Keenes."

"Yes. I have asked the police to give me a list of the priests in Rome named Corso."

"Oh boy," said Ken, "that's a common name around here. It means street. There may be a lot of names on your list."

"I'll bring it in the morning. How about seven o'clock. I rise early."

"Make it eight," pleaded Ken.

"Okay. Eight."

Chapter 20

Thursday, February 21
Day 4, Rome

When we returned to our room following our visit with Monsignor Corso, we found all of the clothes we had ordered laid out on our beds. There were two of the small rolling suitcases, so we were ready to travel. We sat down to think about what we had learned of DaVinci's gold experiments.

"We haven't seen the news for three days," I said as I turned on CNN International. After news of the troop movements in Saudi Arabia to conduct exercises near the Kuwait border, and a giant mud slide in India, a map of Rome with Trastevere printed by the red dot came on the screen.

The newscaster said, "The wave of violence in Europe continued today in the old section of Rome." Then, over pictures of a crime scene in an alley showing police moving among bodies, came a voice, "Three people were killed and another injured in Trastavere."

"Look!" shrieked Lyn, "That's Major Wallis."

"It sure is." We both stared intently at the screen.

"This follows the killings yesterday in the ski resort of Zermatt, Switzerland," the screen now showing the Swiss map with the red dot by Zermatt. "There in a day long string of violence, three police officers, two gunmen, and an American couple were victims of what may be slayings related to those in Rome today. Swiss authorities confirm their Zurich chief of detectives went to Rome to follow up on the murders in Zermatt. The American couple has been identified as Mr. and Mrs. Frank Schultz of Bradforton, Illinois."

"No! No!" cried Lyn. "What have we done?"

"My God," I said. "We got them killed!" We both became hysterical, crying and clinging to each other, sobbing and muttering for several minutes.

Then, uncharacteristically, Lyn announced, "We're going to get the son of a bitch that did this."

"Yes, we owe Beaver and Fran that. But we'll need help. Either Willi or that man from our embassy."

"Maybe both, dear. That Willi is obviously on their tail. Maybe those he killed here in Rome were the ones who murdered Beav and Fran."

"Maybe. That would make me feel better. Why did they all come to Rome. Do you think they were still following us?"

"Probably. Maybe Fran or Beaver told the police about the list with Monsignor Corso's name on it."

"Yes. They could have told them we were on skis and knew our way over the mountain to Italy."

"I hope those Germans didn't torture it out of them."

"Me too, Honey. Should we call Willi's office to see how we can contact him in Rome?"

"No, that seems to always bring the others. Let's just go to our embassy here. Someone there must be aware of our problem."

"Right. Hand me that guidebook. Thanks . . . it says in here they open at 9:00."

"You know, Clark I think we should turn over the list and notebook to them."

"I've got a better idea. Let's have Georgio make copies. We could make enough for all the people on the list. Then they may quit chasing us."

"Good idea. And when the bad guys come to get the list, Major Wallis could catch them and we could rest a little better over Frank and Fran."

"Yeah. I really feel awful about what we caused."

"There was no way to know, Dear. We just have to make sure their killers are punished."

"Georgio comes on duty at 7:00 tomorrow. I'll ask him to get six copies made. We can leave the originals in the safe and take two copies with us to the embassy."

"Should we call them first."

"No, Lyn, let's just go there at 9:00."

Neither of us felt like eating that night. So we went to bed, watched a repeat of the news story the next half hour, and then laid there, silent, in the dark for hours before the muffled sobs became snores.

Chapter 21

Friday, February 22
Day 5, Rome

At 7:00, Georgio was at his desk. To my request to have six copies of the notebook and list ready by 8:30 he said no problem. He would put the originals in the hotel safe and send the copies to our room. "I will have your breakfast sent up now," this marvel of concierges concluded.

"Thank You!" I replied.

At 8:00, Major Wallis and Lieutenant Dante Bazzani arrived at the U.S. Embassy and were escorted to Ken Merrill's office to meet with Ken and Ridley Taylor on how to find the Keenes. Lieutenant Bazani had brought with him a list of priests named Corso. One Monsignor, two bishops, and thirty nine priests.

"I say let's start with the Monsignor," Ridley suggested.

"The lieutenant's office is already working on an appointment with him for later today. He is the curator of the Vatican Museum," Willi announced proudly.

"An important job," Dante added.

"I'm sure," said Merrill. They continued to discuss the case.

At 9:00, the meeting was interrupted when the desk announced a Mr. and Mrs. Keene were in the lobby and wanted to meet with someone about a report of murders they had seen on CNN. While Ken went down to get them, the others decided Major Wallis and Lieutenant Bazzani should go in the adjoining room and listen on the intercom.

"This is our liaison in Switzerland, Ridley Taylor," Ken said as he entered the room. "Rid, meet Clark and Lyn Keene."

"I recognize you," Lyn blurted out. "You were with Major Wallis in Zermatt. Tell us, please, what happened to our friends?"

"We saw on television they were killed," I added.

"Yes. After the initial shootings, they were fine. They went with the major and me to the police station. They told us of the list, and that you may have come here to see this priest, Father Corso."

"We did. It's Monsignor Corso at the Vatican Museum. He is studying the notebook and is to call us today. But, about the Shultzes."

"We felt they needed to be protected, so Willi, that's Major Wallis . . ."

"We know," I interrupted.

"He wanted them protected. He sent two of the Zermatt police back to their home to guard them. Later, we found the Schultzes and the two guards dead. They had all been killed with a knife. Willi thinks it was done by one of the Germans that have been following you. His name is Rudi Heiss. Here is his picture."

"That's the one that grabbed me in the Baur au Lac the other night. He must have killed that other man, too."

"He has killed many people with his stiletto. He is a bad character that is part of a neo-nazi terrorist group called the Aryan Elite."

"Was he one of those killed here in Rome yesterday?" Lyn wanted to know.

"No, but his partner was. One Heinz Ruppert. Here's his picture."

"That's the other one from the hotel," Lyn said pointing at the picture. "That's a start," she went on. "We want to help catch the others who did this to our friends. We feel so responsible."

"You shouldn't feel that way," Ken began. "I've been in police work a long time and can tell you that you are not responsible for the actions of these thugs."

"But if we hadn't gone there," I said.

"They weren't in Zermatt because of you. Major Wallis had a person on his staff that was selling information to several different groups. He has arrested him, so that should stop."

"We suspected he had a 'mole', or whatever you call them. We have been afraid to call."

"He knows that. In fact, he is here now and has been listening to our discussion. Come in Willi, and bring the lieutenant with you."

Willi came in the room and said, "I'm so sorry about your friends. We thought we had them protected. But, as Mr. Merrill said, it is not your fault."

"Do you know where this Rudi is now?" Lyn countered.

"That was the Aryan Elite's Rome safe house we raided yesterday. Unfortunately, Rudi, along with another of their tough guys, Rolf Strang, from Berlin, got away."

"We have a search going on now," the Italian policeman said in heavily accented English.

"Forgive me," Willi offered, "this is Lieutenant Dante Bazzani of the Rome police. He's our host here in Italy."

"Lieutenant," we both acknowledged him.

"We are serious about wanting to help," I said.

"I need to tell you more before you commit. Your government, at the highest levels, wanted us to refuse to let you 'come in out of the cold,' as we call it. They wanted to use you as the bait to catch these people."

"The government?" I asked in awe.

"Yes, in fact, President Bush held a meeting in his office yesterday about your case."

"Incredible," Lyn said.

"The secretaries of state, treasury, and defense were there, along with the Chairman of the Joint Chiefs of Staff and several other advisors, including the director of the CIA."

"What could be so important. Certainly not the notebook or list. Didn't Beaver tell you that the book is about failed attempts to make gold," I said.

Lyn added, "And this list everybody wants is not 'The List', which is actually something from Faust 500 years ago."

I handed out the two copies of the list and notebook we brought along. "Here, see for yourselves."

"You've made copies?" Willi asked.

"Yes. Monsignor Corso made one yesterday to study. As I said, we are to hear from him today. And we had enough copies made for the others on the list. We thought if they had this, they might leave us alone."

"Back to your question of importance," Ridley began again, "besides the Germans, Iraq is involved. They were part of the shoot out in Zermatt. There were also Sicilians, probably Mafia, and there are mining interests from Denver following you about. We think they were not involved in the shootings. They made a $25,000 offer to buy the list."

"We were up above in the woods. We saw the two of you and the other police coming up the path. The Germans were following you. Two others, one of whom looked like Victor Mature, were following the Germans. And one other group was sneaking through the woods on the other side."

"That was probably the Iraqi assassin team."

"It's the Iraq interest that caused the president to get involved. They simply can't take a chance that such a formula exists. If Iraq had such a thing, they would win the war."

"We saw on CNN the movement of our troops closer to the border."

"A related move," said Ken.

"Wow! What do you think Lyn, are we still in?"

"You bet. We're going to find those responsible for the death of our friends."

"You heard her. What can we do to help?"

"Just go on with you plan to meet with those on the list. We'll be watching. If you have a problem, call this number. It's a hot line that is monitored at all hours. We'll continue to look for Heiss and Strang. And we will talk to the Monsignor. Please tell him it is okay to talk to us."

"We will," Lyn said, "We have been staying at the Hotel Senato by the Pantheon. We'll wait there till we hear from Monsignor Corso."

"If he calls this morning," I added, "we will take the afternoon train to Palermo. I checked the schedule this morning. It leaves Termini Station at 12:10 P.M. and gets to Palermo at 11:30 P.M. We will stay at the Jolly Hotel on the waterfront. We've been there before."

Ridley said, "I'll try to be on the same train, but please don't show any form of recognition. That could be bad for both of us."

"All right."

"In Palermo, you will be contacted by a Brother Pietro of the 'Protectors of the Mariners'. He is CIA."

"I will fly to Palermo after we have found Heiss." volunteered the major.

"The local authorities will also know of our strategy," said Dante.

We left the embassy, both excited about finding the killers and about the prospect of serving our country. We also left scared of what might lay ahead. When we got back to the hotel we found a phone message to call Monsignor Corso. When we reached him he was very excited.

"This notebook is like I suspected. The notes of a doctoral student at the university in Heidelberg. The writer thinks Faust was a better alchemist, but he didn't have the more advanced equipment like our Leonardo had designed here in Rome. By using Faust's formula on DaVinci's machine, according to the student, DaVinci could make gold."

"He never did, did he Monsignor?"

"I don't believe anyone ever found those papers of Faust."

"That's our infamous 500 year old list everyone wants," I said.

"Yes, Mr. Keene. I plan to find the old DaVinci materials we have and look there to see if he had a similar list. It will take some time, but I will let you know."

"Thank you, Sir. We have been meeting with the police from here and from Switzerland, along with people from the American Embassy. We are working together, so please share this information with them. They have copies of the notes. I must also warn you that two German thugs are here in Rome and they have your name. There are also assassins from Iraq here who the police believe have been following the Germans. That's what the shooting in Trastevere was about yesterday."

"I'll be careful. I rarely leave the Vatican and we have the best of security here. Our monitoring is constant, and we have the wonderful Swiss Guardsmen."

"The ones in the funny costumes?" I asked.

"Don't let that fool you, my son. They are well trained mercenaries who have sworn to protect the Pope and this property with their lives."

"Thank you, Father, for all your help. If the others do show up, just give them a copy of the notebook and list. That may send them home."

"I'll think about it. Go with God my new friends."

Georgio had confirmed a room at the Jolly and had our seat reservations for the train when we went down with our new luggage. We thanked Georgio for all his help, and he thanked us for the generous tip.

As we were boarding the taxi, he was standing out front saying, "Arivederci, come again."

We found our seats in a new first class car. We were happy to see Ridley across the aisle and up six rows, riding backwards and looking at us. Ken Merrill was with him. About an hour south of Rome, we passed them on our way to the dining car without the slightest recognition. We thought we were getting better at this spy business. The whole trip down to the toe of Italy and across the Straits of Messina on the train ferry was calm. I woke Lyn as we were pulling into the station in Palermo. Only ten minutes late . . . probably a new Italian Rail record.

The streets were quiet that night. We hoped that was an omen of the days ahead, but, given the events of recent days, we knew that was not to be.

Chapter 22

Friday, February 22
Day 5, Rome

After we left the American Embassy in Rome that morning, Ridley, Ken, Willi, and Dante divided up responsibilities. They would first all visit Monsignor Corso to see what he had determined from the notebook. Then Lieutenant Bazzani would place officers outside the museum to see if any of the other parties showed up there. He was then to go back to the Aryan Elite safe house in Trastevere to do a more detailed search.

Ken and Ridley were to accompany us to Palermo while Willi was to further his interrogation of Ulrich Hurd. Then he planned to send his other two officers back to Zurich with Hurd on the police plane. Afterward, he would take the Alitalia flight to Palermo. He figured he would arrive in Palermo first. He would check with the local authorities to see what they knew about this Gaspar Catalbo.

"Thank you, Monsignor Corso, for agreeing to see us on such short notice," Lieutenant Bazzani began. "It is a matter of police urgency."

"The Keenes have explained that you are all cooperating," Father Corso replied. "This is most interesting."

They were all fascinated by him and his interpretation of the notebook. They were also convinced that without "The List" that had been lost for five centuries, everyone was on a wild goose chase.

"I'll have Ambassador Law convince the mining executives of that when he meets with them later today," Ken Merrill said. "Maybe that will get them out of the hunt."

"Good idea, Ken. Have the ambassador give them a copy of the list and notebook. That okay with you, Willi?" asked Ridley.

"Ja. Yes, we need to get some of the parties out of this."

"From what the monsignor says, the Sicilians are not working for the Americans. They must be working for themselves," Rid suggested.

"Yes. The priest said the Mafioso also tried to make gold," added Dante. "They can be very dangerous. I hope your American couple will be careful."

"We'll contact Brother Pietro to see what he knows before they get to Sicily. We can call it off if it looks too dangerous," Ken said.

When they left the Vatican, Ken and Rid returned to the embassy. They briefed the ambassador and then packed so they could catch the train to Palermo. The ambassador agreed to call Washington to bring them up to date. He would meet with Blackmann and O'Brien. He would give them a copy of the notebook and list. Then he would persuade them to return home. When he called Washington, he got Cathy Pagent, who was the only one working early that morning.

Major Wallis went to the central jail where Ulrich Hurd was being held. He got the names of all of his contacts: Rudi Heiss of the Aryan Elite, Yousef Mohammed from Iraq, Vittorio Mancini with the Mafia, and Kermit Blackmann from Denver. He also got the number of Ulrich's bank account where his payoffs had been deposited. Willi called Zurich and had arrest warrants issued for the four contacts. He also got an impound order on the bank account.

Then he called Ken Merrill and caught him just before he and Ridley were leaving for the station. "Tell your ambassador to advise Mr. Blackmann not to return to Switzerland. I have had an arrest warrant issued on him for bribing a police officer."

"We'll tell him, Willi. Thanks!"

Willi then sent his two escorts with Hurd back to Zurich with orders to put him in the maximum security jail until his return. He then flew to Palermo.

Lieutenant Bazzani, along with four members of the Rome antiterrorist squad, returned to the safe house in Trastevere. They entered from both the front and back in a coordinated assault, even though they didn't expect to find anyone there. To their surprise, shots were fired from upstairs as they reached the first floor landing. The squad returned the fire with their automatic, specially made Baretta assault rifles.

They could hear running footsteps up the stairs to the roof. They were in hot pursuit. More shots, single and automatic, rang out in the building. As the first member of the antiterrorist squad reached the roof, a single shot hit him above his left eye. He tumbled lifeless back down the stairs into his comrades.

By the time they got around him, they could see two figures racing across the roof of the next building. Their shots felled one of the two, but the other disappeared over the edge of the building next door. They ran to the ledge. They could see the second assailant had jumped first to a lower roof, then to a garage, and, finally, into the alley below. That person was now rounding the corner into the street that led to the Piazza. There the afternoon crowds would make it impossible to find him or her.

They dragged the wounded assailant back to the stairs where Lieutenant Bazzani was bending over the body of their fellow officer.

"Paolo is dead," he told them.

"This is the one who killed him," shouted one of the others.

"He is an Arab," said another.

"Very interesting," replied Dante. "It seems our Iraqi assassination team has taken up residence in the German's headquarters."

He slapped the man awake. He was dying of two shots to his lungs. He would say nothing. They didn't find any identification on him or in the house. Dante surmised that they must have been waiting for the Germans to return, as they had probably lost their trail. He also figured that the one that got away must be Seraph Najim. He tried to question the Iraqi again, but he was dead. Dante issued an alert to apprehend Seraph Najim. A final search of the house turned up only the Iraqi's clothes and a cache of ammunition. Dante returned to his office and put in a call to the police in Palermo. He asked them to have Major Wallis call him when he arrived. He sent two more officers to the Vatican Museum to watch for the Germans and the lone assassin from Iraq.

Seraph Najim had circled the Piazza. She bought a bright colored Italian silk scarf from one of the stalls in the square. She then returned to the street that ran in front of the safe house. She moved the motor scooter that she and Abdul had rented into the next block. She waited until the fancily dressed policeman who had been at the house both days came out. He talked with the other policemen for a moment. It appeared to Seraph that they were going to wait for other investigators to come to the scene.

The main officer got into a small police car and drove away. She followed him to the station. There she waited for him to come out to go home. She judged he could tell her all she needed to know, since the trail of the Germans was now cold.

Later that afternoon, the lieutenant did leave the station in civilian clothes. She followed his small Fiat Cinquicento to the football stadium, where Rome was playing Milan in soccer that afternoon. After they parked, she stopped him in a remote section of the lot.

"Scuza, Signore, I have a problem with my baby. Help, please. It's right over here." Dante followed her over to a van, where she pulled a gun. "Inside," she commanded. She sat him in the back seat, pulled off her scarf, and said, "You have been looking for me."

Dante gasped as he realized it was Seraph Najim. She screwed a silencer onto her gun and, without warning, shot Bazzani in the right kneecap. The pain was excruciating.

"Now, I want to know, where are the Americans who have the list? And what has become of the Germans?"

"We don't know about the Germans," he gasped through the pain. "We think they will try to see Monsignor Corso at the Vatican Museum. He has the list, but it is useless. I have a copy in my car. The Americans are gone."

"Pffffl," the silenced gun sounded as she shot him in the other knee. "Not good enough," she said.

He told her they had gone to Palermo to another name on the list, one Gaspar Catalbo. He said the Swiss policeman had gone there also, but he didn't tell her about the CIA.

She had heard enough. Her next shot was between Dante's eyes. She took his car keys and found his copy of the list and notebook. She decided to return to the city in his car, as it would be more comfortable. She drove to the Vatican Museum. She could see it was closed. There were at least four police officers watching the entrance, so she decided to find a phone and call Baghdad for instructions.

General Hanfi congratulated her on her excellent work in getting the list. She told him the notebook was in German. The general told her to go on to Palermo. He would meet her there at noon tomorrow.

"In front of the opera house at noon," he said. "I will bring someone who can read the German."

She told him of the deaths of her squad and the others.

"No matter," he replied. "They died in an important cause. They will be honored in the eyes of Allah and our leader, Saddam Hussein. I will tell him of your valor."

"Thank you, General. I will see you in Palermo."

Rudi Heiss and Rolf Strang also saw the police officers in front of the museum entrances. They went around the back and scaled a wall, dropping into the Vatican gardens. On the far side, they saw a large group of priests and nuns walking with a taller man dressed in white. It was after 5:00 so they assumed it was the Pope taking a walk.

They were concerned they would be seen so they kept close to the walls, behind the shrubbery and trees. At the base of the gardens they came to a six story building they figured to be the museum. They found a door, forced it open, and went up the stairs inside. They looked into each floor. The first five opened into dark corridors or rooms. The sixth door, marked "5", as the lowest level would be the ground floor, opened into a large work area. There was a glassed-in office at the far end with the lights on. A priest with white hair and a beard was studying at his desk. The two crept silently to the office door.

"Come in. I have been expecting you."

What Rudi and Rolf didn't know was that they had been seen coming over the garden wall on the Swiss Guard video monitors. They also triggered a silent alarm when they forced open the door.

"What?" Rudi shouted. "Where are the Americans with my list?"

"They are gone. They told me you would come for the list and a notebook. They asked me to give you a copy in the hope that you would stop chasing them. It is a true copy, I can assure you."

The two were dumbfounded. Rudi grabbed the papers and stuffed them in his shirt. They were considering what to do with the priest when all the lights in the main room went on.

Three Swiss Guardsmen were charging towards the office. Rudi dove out of the office and rolled behind a work table. Rolf came through the door shooting at the guards and wounding one. Rolf was then hit in the chest by a shot from much closer range. Rudi knew it was his chance to rid himself of the danger Rolf's presence posed. He took it, and shot. The guards were somewhat confused by that shot. This gave Rudi the opening to shoot the remaining two guards and run to the door.

All of a sudden, he heard more guards coming up the stairwell. He ran to the other side of the room and went through a curtained archway. He found himself in the museum at the top of the double circular ramps that moved visitors in and out of the building in large numbers. The ramps were intertwined so that those going up never met those coming down. Rudi took the down ramp. As he was descending, he could see guards running up the other ramp. Just before he reached the bottom, he jumped over the rail into a dark corner. There, in a wall panel, he could see an opening through which the guards had probably come. He slipped through the opening and found himself in the Basilica. There were large crowds there. He joined a German tour group and went with them the rest of the way through St. Peter's. He even rode with them on their bus to their next stop at the ancient Castel San Angelo.

He found a pay phone and called Max Bormann in Berlin. "I have the list!" he announced proudly, "and a notebook, too."

"That's good, Rudi," Max exclaimed.

"Rolf is dead, Max. Killed just now by the guards at the Vatican."

"Oh, no," cried Bormann. Max had been his best enforcer. They were also lovers. "But you have the list. What does it say?"

"It is a list of names. One is Monsignor Corso, who gave us the list. There is a Gunter Siegrist in Staufen, Professor Schnelling at Heidelberg, Gaspar Catalbo in Palermo, a Countess Von Anton in Corfu, and Kermit Blackmann in some place called Denver."

"Very interesting. You have a notebook, too?"

"Yes, Max. It is in formal, old German. Full of formulas and lists."

"Good, Rudi. It may be what we are looking for. Bring it to me here in Berlin. Too bad about Rolf. But good work, Rudi. I will move you to Berlin headquarters where you will take Rolf's place."

Rudi hung up the phone soaring with pride. He was now one step from being the world leader of the Aryan Elite. Shooting Rolf during the gun battle had proven to be a master stroke. "I'm good," Rudi thought, "I'm good."

He would fly to Berlin on the next flight. He would need papers and different clothes. As he left the phone booth he saw a young priest walking alone. "My size," Rudi thought as he fell in behind the priest.

Chapter 23

Saturday, February 23
Day 6, Palermo

The sun was brilliant, reflecting off the Conca d'Oro, Palermo's Gulf of Gold. It was already 8:30 and Lyn was still asleep as I went out on the balcony. The fishing boats were at work just off the shore and the ferry from Sardinia was making its way into port off to my left.

I re-entered the room and woke Lyn saying, "It's a beautiful day. Sunny and warm."

"Not till I have breakfast, it isn't," she yawned.

I called room service and asked them to send up some fresh fruit, cornettos, tea for me, and hot chocolate for Lyn.

"How will we find this Gaspar person, Clark?"

"They said we would be contacted by Brother Pietro, who is CIA. So we wait."

Breakfast arrived a few minutes later and the waiter set it up on the balcony. I hadn't paid much attention, but when he came back into the room he asked, "You two okay?"

"It's you, Ridley Taylor. When did you start working as a waiter?"

"This morning. Your real waiter liked my tip better than what he expected from you."

"What do we do next?" Lyn wanted to know.

"A small change of plan. You are to go to Gaspar's Bar at noon. It's on the waterfront by the ferry terminal on Via Francesco Crespi. Take a table and Brother Pietro will make contact."

"Is that our Gaspar that runs the bar?" I asked.

"Yes, it is the hangout for sailors when they are in port. It can get rough at night, but you should be all right at noon. Gaspar is the contact man for the chief Mafia don, Emilio Corleone."

"There really is such a person?"

"Oh yes. There is a village in the mountains above here named Corleone. That's where he lives."

Ridley went on to tell us that Major Wallis had arrived last evening before us and had checked with the local police. "They told Willi that the Don was a very approachable and honorable person. They said if you were bringing him something he wanted he would probably grant you a meeting and safe passage. Brother Pietro is trying to arrange such a meeting through Gaspar. He will fill you in when you meet."

"Sounds exciting." Lyn said.

"We hope to be able to follow you. But you must be careful. These are dangerous people. Are you sure you want to go?"

"Yes," I replied, "we have to know if they had anything to do with the death of our friends."

"Take this small silent beeper. If anything goes wrong, press this button. It will start sending a silent locator signal to us. Good Luck!"

After he was gone I said to Lyn, "Well, is this enough adventure for you?"

She grinned and replied, "Can you believe it? We're going to meet with the head of the Mafia? Emilio Corleone. Nobody back in Cape Elizabeth is going to believe us."

I studied the tourist map I had gotten from the concierge and found Via Francesco. Then we checked on schedules to Corfu, as that seemed the next logical stop in our quest. To fly, it meant changes in both Rome and Athens. There was a train back to the mainland and then across the bottom of the boot to Brindisi, where we could catch a ferry. While we felt safer with the train, the journey including the ferry would take almost two days. So we had the concierge hold space for us on the flight leaving Palermo at 8:00 the next morning. The connections would get us to Corfu by 3:00 on Sunday afternoon.

The concierge called back to say he had made arrangements for the flights on a tentative basis. He also said he would hold our room for tonight. He told us the hotel shuttle would leave for downtown at 11:30. It would drop us off by the opera house, the Teatro Massimo, ten minutes later.

We had about an hour and a half to wait so we took a long walk along the Foro Umberto, which runs along the shore. We stopped at some old ruins and in the Botanical Gardens. We didn't talk much, as each of us, in our own way, was still grieving over the loss of our friends. We were wondering if we were doing the right thing. At 11:15 we returned to the hotel, got a copy of the list and notebook from our room, and boarded the van.

We were dropped off on the side of the square which fronted the opera. The driver said he returned to the Jolly every hour on the hour. We crossed the square and started walking down the Via Cavour toward the harbor. We didn't notice the three people sitting on a bench on the far side of the stone square.

One of them noticed us. It was Seraph Najim, and she said to the others, "I'm glad you were early, General. Allah has smiled upon us. That is the American couple who had the list coming across the plaza. I recognize them from the pictures the Italian policeman had in his briefcase."

"They must be here to see this Gaspar on the list," General Hanfi stated, "Let us follow them. Achmed, you can study the notebook later."

We also hadn't noticed the four men in a car that had followed our van from the hotel. Willi, Ridley, Ken, and their plainclothes Palermo police escort, Alphonso Ricci. They saw the three Arabs rise and start to follow us. Rid and Willi jumped from the car and went after them. Ken and Officer Ricci drove down the Via Roma and then over to Via Cavour to cut them off. They enlisted the help of two patrolmen who were watching for pickpockets at the busy intersection where these two major shopping streets meet.

As we past an opening, the three Arabs caught us and pushed us into the alley.

"Mr. and Mrs. Keene, I believe," said the woman who had the look of death about her, even through her beautiful dark eyes.

"We want all you have about this list of gold," the older man said, "and we want it now!"

"I think not," Ridley exclaimed while pointing his pistol at Seraph.

"You are all under arrest," said Willi.

The arrest went very smoothly, without a single shot fired. Seraph had started to pull her gun, when Ridley grabbed her wrist from behind. His vice-like grip pinned her arms. Neither the general nor the translator had a weapon, as they had just come from the airport. They took them to the maximum security prison. There, Taylor and Merrill, on behalf of the United States, made a formal request that they be charged with espionage. As Italy was a member of the Coalition, they said that would not be a problem. Ken Merrill went to a phone to call Bryan Roberts in Washington.

A number of shoppers had witnessed the arrest. One of them slipped away and went down the street into an alley. He went in the back door of Gaspar's.

While that was going on, we found the front entrance to Gaspar's Bar. We took a table by the front window and ordered two local beers.

Shortly after we entered, a rotund, jovial man in a monk's tunic came in and started touring all the tables. He was expressing happiness to all and passing out prayer cards. There was a group of Spanish sailors off a warship from Spain at the bar. They tried to joke with the monk and started to jostle him. Very deftly he sat each one in turn back firmly on their stool.

He approached our table and said, "Buon journo, Signore, Signora."

"Buon journo!" Lyn replied.

"Good afternoon," was my response.

"Oh," said the monk, "Americans. Sounds like Boston. I'm from Chicago myself."

"Actually, it's Maine. Near Portland, but only a hundred miles north of Boston," I said.

"I pride myself on accents. What brings you to Sicily?" Before we could answer, he added, "Vacation, no doubt. Well it's a beautiful place. Rich in history. The Greeks, Romans, Moors, Etruscans: they were all here. And the Crusaders. There is a Norman Cathedrale in Cefalu. Well, I have to go. More souls to save, you know. You have my blessing, fellow countrymen."

With that he left a prayer card on the table and he was out the door. I looked at the card and turned it over. It had a note which read, "Gaspar will come to your table in five minutes. Everything is set. It's okay."

In exactly five minutes, a slender man dressed in slacks and a navy sweater came to our table. "I am Gaspar, owner of this establishment. Would you like another beer? It's on the house."

"Thank you," I said.

"We don't get many Americans in here. Just your sailors when they are in port for recreation. This place can sometimes get rough. I think you would enjoy your beer more, and perhaps some lunch, in my dining room in the back."

We followed him through a partition at the back of the bar. We were in a dining room, but it looked like it had been closed for some time. Two men emerged from the shadows in the corner.

"It's okay," Gaspar said, "You will not be harmed. We understand you have something for the Don."

"Yes," I stuttered feebly.

"This is Nick and Sammy. They will drive you to your meeting with Don Corleone. But first I must asked you to empty your pockets onto the table."

They searched us and Lyn's travel bag for weapons. The only thing they took was the silent alarm beeper. "You won't be needing this. Besides, your followers are now busy at the prison with the Arabs who were following you here. In any event I will have someone drive this button toward Segesta. You will not need help."

"May I ask you something, Gaspar?" I said as I picked up the list, "Why is your name on this list?"

"I don't know, except all who talk to the Don must go through me. He may explain further. Go."

We went out the back door, where there was a large Lincoln limousine parked in the alley. We heard the rear doors lock as our two silent escorts got in the front and we drove away.

"At least our protectors got the Iraqis," I said.

"Yes, I'm happy about that, Clark. But it means they're not with us now."

"We'll be okay, honey. These people may be gangsters, but they have a code of honor. So if the Don gave us safe passage, we'll be okay."

Once out of the city, we began to climb. In about thirty minutes we pulled in to the village of Monreale. We stopped in front of the famous 12th century Cathedral of Santa Maria la Nuova. We had visited the church the last time we were in Palermo. We both remembered it as having the most beautiful mosaics we had ever seen. The sign said in several languages that the shrine was closed from 1:00 until 3:00.

It was past one, but the door swung open as we approached. We both immediately recognized the man that met us. It was "Victor Mature" from the shoot out in Zermatt. My back stiffened in fear and anger. He dismissed the two drivers with a wave of his hand and asked us to follow him. We walked through the empty church. The sunlight played on the mosaics and almost gave them life.

We went behind the alter and through a doorway into a large waiting room which was furnished like an office. A man about my age, sixty or so, with a full head of graying hair, rose from the desk to greet us. He was wearing a very expensive blue Italian silk suit with a silver silk tie. Central casting sure had this one right.

"Welcome. I am Emilio Corleone. It is nice of you to come. Please have a seat." He directed us to a sofa and then sat in a leather winged back chair across a small coffee table from us. There was a silver coffee service on the table. "I understand, Mr. Keene, that you like tea. So do I," he said as he poured two cups. "And for you, lovely lady, I have hot chocolate. I know you have not had any lunch. My chef is fixing us some sea bass in rock salt. It is magnificent and should be ready shortly. Anthony, you may leave us. We'll be all right." Tony Ruffini left us alone with the Don.

"Now to business," said the Don. "You have questions for me?"

"Yes Sir," I started.

Lyn interrupted, "But first I must know this. The man who just left the room. He was in Zermatt. Did he murder our friends?"

"No, Mrs. Keene, Anthony did not kill your friends. From what we have learned, it was a German, Rudi Heiss, that was responsible. Tony only killed one of the other Germans that was there. Too bad he missed Heiss. I express my sympathy to you both over the loss of the Schultzes."

"Thank you, Mr. Corleone. We will be happy to share our information with you," Lyn replied.

"Please, my name is Emlio. And may I call you by your first names?"

"Certainly," I said. I started with our finding of the notebook and list. "Here is a copy of each you may keep. We are told they are not worth very much. A student of chemistry at Heidelberg University compiled them while doing his Doctoral Thesis on the black art of alchemy. The making of gold from other metals. The notebook is his research. The list is of people he wanted to talk to in order to complete the thesis. You'll note the name of Gaspar Catalbo on the list. That is why we are here."

"Very interesting. Gaspar would know little about our experiments. He is on the list as a conduit to me. You see Faust and DaVinci on the list. Hundreds of years ago, padrones in my position sought the secret of making gold from lead. I joke that you can only do that if the lead is in the form of bullets in a gun."

Lyn giggled behind me.

"We had copies of the DaVinci work papers from the Vatican. No one, we believe, ever found Dr. Faust's notes. For over two centuries, my predecessors hired the great chemists of their time to carry on the experiments. All to no avail. It simply can't be done."

"That agrees with all we have learned, Emilio."

"Yes, but when we learned you had found a list, we couldn't chance that it was not the one of Faust. That is why I sent Anthony to find out. Thank you for bringing these papers to me. It solves the mystery."

"Do you have any idea why these other names are on the list?" Lyn asked.

"We talked about Faust and DaVinci. That would cover Gunter Siegrist and Monsigor Corso at the top. I don't know about Professor Schnelling. I have not heard that Heidelberg University ever conducted experiments. I would know that, unless they are recent. Gaspar is on the list to learn of our studies. Kermit Blackmann at the bottom is a similar thing. His company, Denver Mining, along with others in the gold mining business, has done experiments like ours. Again, without success. If I can be frank, their motives and ours are not that different. If we could make gold we could use it to control the world's financial markets. Our funds would be handled by every major bank without concern. The mining companies already control the gold supply, so they control those markets now. They experiment to make sure that we, or anybody else, can't make gold. They are protecting what they have, and what the rest of us want. Finally, this Countess von Anton in Corfu, I have no idea why she is on the list. I believe it was her ancestor, a Baron Anton, who employed Faust."

"Thank you, Sir. That is very helpful," I concluded.

Lunch was served on the terrace overlooking the valley and the city below. The sea bass was better that any fish either of us had ever eaten. The wine was a delicate white Regaleali which was superb. Conversation during lunch was about grandchildren. Lyn and Emilio exchanged pictures. He also talked of wines and flowers, and the need for more employment opportunities in Sicily.

After a scrumptious torte di limone, Anthony appeared from somewhere. We said our good-byes and were escorted back to the Lincoln. In the car on the way back to town Lyn said,

"What a nice, cultured person."

"Be careful, Honey. He may be charming, but I sure wouldn't want to cross him."

After several minutes of silence Lyn whispered, "Do you suppose the countess is on our list because she has the Faust list?"

"Could be. Let's go ask her."

As the Don and Tony Rufini got in their Ferrari Roadster for the drive back to Corleone, the Don said, "Tony, you should go to Corfu. Just to make certain the Countess von Anton does not have the list of Dr. Faust. No rough stuff. Just find out what she tells the Keenes. Capiece?"

"Yes, Padrone, I understand."

Chapter 24

Saturday, February 23
Day 6, Various

After leaving the prison, Ken Merrill had gone after the locator beeper out on the highway past the airport toward Segesta. Ridley Taylor contacted Brother Pietro and found the Keenes had already met with Corleone. He assured Rid that everything was okay.

Taylor called Merrill on his cellular and told him to return to Palermo. They would meet at the Jolly with Major Wallis and the local police. While Rid waited, he called Ambassador Law.

The ambassador told Ridley that Mr. Blackmann and Mr. O'Brien were happy to have the notebook and list. They were sure they were of no value, but they would verify that back in Denver. They had reminded the ambassador that they wanted to cooperate in this matter. It was in the best interests of the United States to protect the integrity of the gold supply at Fort Knox. The ambassador was waiting for a return call from Washington. He wanted to check with Secretary Brady at the treasury to see if he would meet with Blackmann and O'Brien.

"I also told them to stay out of Switzerland. We didn't want to have to get them out of jail."

"That's good, Sir. Do you think they'll go home?"

"They hope to leave later today to meet with Brady on Monday."

"Okay. We'll stay in touch."

When Merrill and Wallis arrived they checked with the concierge and found that the Keenes were in their room.

Ken and Ridley had the concierge book them on the 10:00 Sunday flight to Corfu. Willi decided to return to Zurich to oversee the questioning of those arrested in the Ulrich Hurd matter.

"I think after Corfu, they must go to Heidelberg or Staufen. I will rejoin you there."

"Okay, Willi. We have your number and will let you know when we are moving again.

✤ ✤ ✤ ✤ ✤ ✤

Rudi Heiss had arrived in Berlin and was very pleased with the reception he received from Max Bormann. They gave the notebook to a scholar Max had recruited. He wanted a complete and accurate translation.

Max asked Rudi three times to describe the way Rolf was killed and whether he had suffered. Rudi didn't notice, but each time he repeated the story, Max became more distraught. Actually, Max was beginning to suspect there was more to it, as each telling of the story had small details different from the previous versions.

"I must watch Rudi," he thought, while Rudi was thinking how easy it was going to be to reach his career goal.

The scholar returned to ask for more time. They ordered him to work through the night and report in the morning.

✤ ✤ ✤ ✤ ✤ ✤

When Washington heard about the capture of General Hanfi, they were ecstatic. They told Ken Merrill to remain in Palermo. They were sending the top interrogators from the military, along with a team from the agency headed by Bryan Roberts. They wanted everything they could get on the location and movements of Saddam Hussein and his troops. The head of Hussein's Secret Service was the highest ranking officer yet captured during the conflict.

When Saddam learned of the capture that night, he asked his son-in-law, who was head of the Palace Guard, to send two of his trained Italian mercenaries to Palermo. Their orders were to kill General Hanfi and the other two who had brought such disgrace to this holy war.

✤ ✤ ✤ ✤ ✤ ✤

Ridley called Clark on the house phone and then they all met in the bar. Over cocktails, Clark and Lyn told of their meeting with Corleone.

Ken outlined the capture of the Iraqis and the plan for the interrogation team to arrive in the morning. Rid told them that after he had a chance to meet with Bryan Roberts, who was leading the team coming from Washington on Sunday, he would be following them to Corfu on Monday.

After dinner alone in the hotel dining room, which was full with a tour group from Japan, Lyn and Clark went back to their room.

"I just can't get over the thought that we are responsible for the deaths of Fran and Beaver."

"Neither can I, Honey. But the closer we get to finding their killer, the better I feel. I never thought of myself as a vengeful person, but I want Rudi Heiss dead."

"I feel the same way, Dear. Perhaps we'll learn more in Corfu."

"Or will it become another battleground in our quest?" asked Clark.

Chapter 25

Sunday, February 24
Day 7, Corfu

We had set the alarm for 6:00 in order to make our 8:00 flight out of Palermo. When I awoke to the alarm, I could hear Lyn already in the shower. I was going to have to wait my turn for the bathroom, so I turned on CNN International. Scenes of tanks rolling through the desert came on the screen. Bernard Shaw's voice was describing the beginning of the land invasion of Kuwait by the Coalition Forces. He was saying the troops had met with very little resistance from Hussein's army. The southern units were already within thirty miles of Kuwait City. The northern units were trying to close the roads leading back into Iraq.

Lyn came into the room asking, "What's going on?"

"Our Army has started the liberation of Kuwait, Honey."

"We had a little something to do with that, didn't we, Clark?"

"Yes, perhaps we did. I feel very proud right now."

"Me too."

She continued to watch and yell in to me a blow by blow while I showered and dressed. We had the rolls, tea, and hot chocolate the hotel had sent up. Then we took a taxi to the airport.

We didn't notice the U.S. Air Force Lear jet parked on the remote side of the field as we took off on our flight to Rome.

We arrived in Corfu on time after our three flight trip. We both took some melatonin to try to rest. I did sleep on the leg from Rome to Athens. Lyn was wide awake the whole time. The cause, of course, was our excitement over our meeting with Don Emilio Corleone, the invasion in Kuwait, and now searching for Countess Liesel Von Anton.

As we entered the arrival hall, we were approached by a taxi driver complete with a Greek fisherman's cap.

"You look American," he said with a Brooklyn accent.

"Yes," I replied cautiously.

"I am the best driver on the island. Been here eight years. I know everyone and all the best places. I will be your private driver for $125 U.S. dollars a day. Okay?"

"Do you know a Countess Von Anton?" Lyn asked.

"Liesel. Yes, I know her. I have driven for her many times."

"Okay," I said, "You're hired. We came to see her, but we don't know her."

"I, Nicholas Vosnos, that's me, can arrange it."

We got in his ten-year-old Cadillac, which was very clean, and drove away from the airport down to the road along the east coast of the island. Nick, as he wanted to be called, talked constantly. He explained that his grandfather had left three acres of growing grapes and a small house to him in his will. In order to inherit the vineyard, Greek law required him to move to Corfu and live on the land. It wasn't enough to support him, hence, the taxi business.

We were headed toward the main town of Kerkira, or Corfu Town, along a sweeping bay where the waves were crashing on the rock strewn beach. About half way around the bay, Nick pulled over.

"There is the villa of the countess and her friends."

"Her friends?" Lyn asked.

"Yes, she has converted the villa into four apartments. There have been three wealthy, older dowagers living with her for several years. It pays her taxes, she says. I say she loves the company."

"Do you know who they are, Nick?" I questioned.

"Yes, I drive for all of them. There is Barbara Williams from New York. An ex-showgirl who married a wealthy Greek ship owner. He died shortly after they were married. She has lived with the countess for over ten years. Donna Nickels is from London. She is the heiress to the Bass Beer family. Been here seven years. The newcomer, at six years tenure, is Virginia Rufer, from Switzerland. Owns a large amount of the Nestle company stock. They are all wonderful women. Very generous with their tips."

"We'll try to remember that when we settle up, Nick. Right now we need to find a hotel," Lyn yawned.

"Let me take you to the Palace. It's right around the curve, just short of town."

The Corfu Palace proved to be very nice. It was not yet their season, so they had a room available. We were on the third floor. We looked out over the roof of the lobby and restaurant toward the Adriatic. We could see the coastline of Greece to the right and Albania to the left. There were ferry boats running in both directions.

The hotel had sent up some hard rolls, tea, and Lyn's hot chocolate. We devoured that and Lyn was soon asleep. Nick said he would call the countess to ask if she would see us. I told him to tell her it concerned her family in Staufen. He called our room at 6:00 to say the countess would like us to join her and her friends for tea at 4:00 P.M. the next afternoon, and that he would pick us up at 3:45.

That evening we walked into the town and had a wonderful pizza at a cafe facing a large park and the ruins of an old fort.

The next day we slept late, relaxed by the hotel pool, and took a swim. We were in the lobby at 3:40 when Nick pulled up.

"Here we go again," Lyn said as we climbed into the car.

Chapter 26

Sunday, February 24
Day 7, Various

Bryan Roberts and the debriefing team had arrived in Palermo at 6:30. They were all excited about the ground offensive in Kuwait. It made their interrogation of the Iraqis that much more urgent.

They asked the pilots of the air force Lear jet to wait while they went with Ridley Taylor, Ken Merrill, and the local police to the prison to get General Hanfi, Seraph Najim, and the other Iraqi. They planned to fly them to the U.S. air base at Wiesbaden, Germany. There, just outside Frankfurt, they could keep the prisoners secure in the military prison.

Taylor and Merrill met with Roberts while the prisoners were being prepared for transport. They all agreed the use of the Keenes was going better than expected. They also agreed to stay with the plan and have Ridley join the Keenes in Corfu.

The two Italian mercenaries Saddam Hussein's son-in-law had selected were at the Palermo airport and had seen the American plane land. They witnessed the two military officers and three civilians being met by two other Americans and local police officers. They assumed they were going into Palermo to pick up the prisoners, and that they probably would bring them back to the airport to fly them to a POW camp. Their best opportunity to carry out their mission would be here at the airport. They took up strategic positions and waited. One was on the roof of the hanger closest to the plane. The other was behind a fuel depot next to the gate through which the cars had exited.

Two hours later, a convoy of police cars and a convict transfer van approached the gate. It came through and pulled up to the plane. They had it in a cross fire position. After the policemen got out of their cars, they formed a cordon to the plane. Then the van doors were opened. General Hanfi emerged first, followed by Achmed, his German translator, and Seraph Najim.

When all three were outside the van and the general was starting up the plane's stairs, the two gunmen opened fire with their automatic weapons. The general, his translator, and three of the police officers were killed in the first volley. Ken Merrill was also hit in the chest. Bryan Roberts grabbed him as he fell. He punched his fist into Ken's wound to stop the bleeding. The police began to return fire but they were caught in the middle.

Another policeman and one of the military interrogators were in front of Seraph Najim. They took the bullets meant for her. She grabbed the dying policeman's gun with both of her handcuffed hands. Calmly, amid the hail of bullets, she picked out the shooter on the roof and put a shot in his right eye. Then she rolled over the body of the military officer and shot the other assailant as she rose to one knee. She then dove into the plane and pointed the gun at the pilot.

"Fly now!" she screamed as she pulled the door closed. Amid shots being fired at the plane, they took off. Seraph sat down behind the pilot and said, "To Amman Jordan, Infidel."

She knew Iraq's air space was controlled by the coalition forces and she wasn't sure of her own status there. She knew the two assailants had been sent to kill them all so they wouldn't talk. She also figured the plane would not be attacked over Jordan's sovereign space. She was right.

One and a half hours later they touched down in Amman. Seraph called Saddam's son-in-law who had sent the mercenaries. They agreed that she knew more about this operation than anyone. She was to rest overnight. Tomorrow he would come to Jordan and they could provide what she needed to go to Heidelberg to interview Professor Schnelling on Tuesday.

Simultaneously, in Berlin, the scholar had finished his report to Max Bormann and Rudi Heiss.

"My conclusion is that there is no real list or method for making gold; it is a fantasy."

"That may be, but we must be certain," Max said. "Rudi, I have asked our world council to meet with us by teleconference tomorrow afternoon. I want to introduce you to them and have you make a full report on this entire affair. Then, Tuesday, I want you to go to Heidelberg. Find out what this Professor Schnelling might know."

"Yes, Max. I am honored to address the council. I will make plans to take the train to Heidelberg."

Bryan Roberts contacted the director of his agency at his home in Potomac, Maryland. He told him of the ambush and of losing their prisoners and the plane.

"Get things wrapped up in Palermo. Then go up to Wiesbaden and catch a military flight home. All hell is breaking loose here with the ground war in progress. Is Ken going to be okay?"

"The doctors removed the slug and say he has better than an even chance. They will know more tomorrow."

✤ ✤ ✤ ✤ ✤ ✤

Kermit Blackmann and Ned O'Brien were on their way to Washington. They had an appointment with Treasury Secretary Brady the next afternoon.

✤ ✤ ✤ ✤ ✤ ✤

Ridley Taylor and Tony Rufini were separately making plans for their Monday fiights to Corfu. They were both on the 10:00 Alitalia shuttle to Rome.

All of the players were still active in the hunt.

Chapter 27

Monday, February 25
Day 8, Corfu

We rang the countess's doorbell at exactly 4:00. It was answered by an elderly Greek in butler's tails. "Please come in. My name is Dimitrios. The countess is expecting you."

"Thank you," I replied.

"This way, please."

We followed him to an upstairs terrace overlooking the sea. It had been transformed into a lovely rock and flower garden. The countess and her friends were seated on cushioned wrought iron chairs around a matching coffee table. It was loaded with sweets and a large silver tea service.

"Mr. and Mrs. Keene. Welcome. You bring some excitement to our usually drab afternoon tea."

I noticed none of the four were drinking tea. Three of them had something that looked like sherry and one had white wine.

"Please sit," she continued, "here, on the sofa." The matching love seat was positioned on the far side of the table so all four of them were facing us. "These are my friends." She introduced Barbara Williams from New York, Donna Nickels from London, and Virginia Rufer from Geneva.

Each one, in turn, peered over their glasses to utter, "Mr. and Mrs. Keene," with an obvious look of curiosity.

"Your driver, Nicky, tells me you have something concerning my family. But first, may I offer you some tea or wine. And, please, an afternoon sweet. I have a wonderful Black Forrest torte. Or English shortbread cookies. Or local peaches and cream?"

"Thank you, Countess. I'll have the shortbread cookie and tea," I replied.

Lyn said, "I'll have the Black Forrest. It looks scrumptious. And white wine, please."

The ladies looked happy with Lyn's order. We waited while the countess cut the cake and served the cookies and drinks. As she poured my tea, she asked, "One lump, or two?"

"None, thank you." I declined.

She settled back in her chair and looked expectantly at us, indicating it was time for us to begin our story. So, we told them of finding of the list and notebook. Lyn gave her one of the copies we had made in Rome. She glanced at the list and then set it aside. We told them of the chase and the potential danger to her. Her expression didn't change. Then we told her the notebook was about Dr. Faust's time in Staufen in the 16th century.

To that she said, "It was my ancestor, the fourth Baron Anton von Staufen that brought Faust to the village."

"Do you know why?" Lyn asked.

"He needed money, according to our family stories. The money lenders in Frieburg and Basle were pressing him for payments. He had the false hope that Faust could make gold. But then, that was the middle ages and people had a lot of false notions."

"We believe that all of the interest in pursuing this list is to find Faust's records. Some believe they are still hidden in Staufen. Perhaps in the Hotel Zum Lowen. Does your family still own the hotel?" I asked.

"We did at that time," she answered. "The story is that there was an explosion when the townspeople tried to get rid of Faust. The hotel was severely damaged. The baron sold it to a wine growing family, by the name of Knopfel, from Grunern. They had it rebuilt and turned it into the Gasthaus Zum Lowen with a larger weinstube for the sale of their wines. I think the Knopfels may have sold it again very recently, but I am not certain of that."

"This is exciting," said Virginia.

"Do you have any old hotel records?" Barbara asked.

"Yes, Liesel, you may have the formula for making gold!" chirped Donna.

"Be calm, Girls," the countess said, "I have no records. I'm sure if our family had any, they were destroyed years and years ago. The castle has been in ruins for 350 years."

Then the countess turned back to us and said, “I’m sorry I cannot be of more help. Perhaps the Knopfel family has some records. They still have the winery in Grunern.”

“That’s a big help, Countess. Lyn and I will go and see them.”

“Will you also be seeing the others like Gunter Siegrist who is on your list?”

“Yes, we want to see everyone to see what they know and to warn them of the danger of having their name on the list. If you like, we will let you know what we find.”

“Yes, please. That would be entertaining for all of us, we don’t have much to excite us anymore.”

“You all appear to be enjoying life,” Lyn said.

The other three began to talk about the “old days.” Lyn carried on some small talk with them while I wrote down the names of Knopfel and Grunern.

Then, as we prepared to leave, I said, “I don’t want to frighten you, but there are some very sinister people who have copies of this list with your name on it. You may want to consider leaving Corfu until this is resolved.”

“No. We are safe here. No one comes to the island that we don’t hear about. My man, Dimitrios, has friends who will protect us. I will also ask the local authorities to keep watch. Thank you for your concern.”

✣ ✣ ✣ ✣ ✣ ✣

While we had been talking, Ridley Taylor and Toni Rufini were in separate phone booths at the Corfu airport looking up the address of the countess. Then they caught separate taxis.

She rose, as did we. We said our good-byes to the others, thanked the countess again, and followed the butler back to the front door where Nick was waiting. As we were pulling out, another taxi stopped across the street and Ridley got out. We told Nick to pull up behind the taxi. We got out and told Ridley about our visit with the countess.

Lyn watched a third cab go by and said, “That was the Mafia guy that looks like Victor Mature.”

“Yes,” Rid said, “He was on my plane. Obviously, the Don wants to see what you find out.”

We told him again of our visit with Corleone and that he had agreed to take a more passive role.

“Maybe not,” Rid replied.

“You must protect these ladies,” Lyn said.

"I'll contact the local police," Rid answered, "and I'll stay here until they come."

"We're going to Staufen next to see a wine family named Knopfel. The countess says they may have the old hotel records."

"Okay. Where are you staying here?"

"Just down the road at the Palace," Lyn answered.

"Wait there. When the police get here, I'll come there and we can all go to Germany together."

We went on to the Palace. We booked three seats on a Lufthansa flight that was nonstop to Frankfurt from Corfu at 11:00 tomorrow. Then we went to the hotel bar to wait for Ridley. At 9:00, when he hadn't arrived, we called the number the countess had given us. A local policeman answered.

Chapter 28

After we left Ridley in front of the Countess Von Anton's villa, he went to the door and rang the bell. He showed the butler his U.S. Embassy official's identification and said he had additional information from the Keenes. The butler had seen him talking to us in front of the villa. He asked him to wait in the hall while he checked with the countess. He returned in a few minutes to say that she would see him. He followed Dimitrios to the terrace where afternoon "tea" was still being imbibed by the four dowagers. In fact, after the excitement of our story, the "tea" had switched from sherry and wine to gin and brandy.

He showed his credentials to the countess. She said, without offering tea, "You have more information from the Keene's?"

Ridley replied, "Yes. I saw them as they were leaving your villa. We have been working together and I arrived on a flight today. As we were speaking, a Mafia gunman from Sicily drove past. He had been on my plane. I'm convinced he is here to see what you told the Keenes."

"I told them very little," the countess said.

"I know. The Keenes filled me in on your conversation. We are concerned for your safety. I would like to call the local police to post a guard."

"That shouldn't be necessary. My man, Dimitrios, has connections with people who can protect us. They speak the Mafia's language."

At that moment, Tony Rufini stepped on to the terrace from behind a trellis of roses, not yet in bloom, at the far end. He had apparently scaled the rock face of the steep hill that closed in that end of the house. He had a gun in his hand. He asked Ridley to place his gun on the table and to step back. He also called the Butler into the open from the doorway into the house.

The countess's three friends were all breathing rapidly, but Liesel remained calm.

"I do not intend to harm you, Ladies. I just want to know what you told the Keenes."

"Very little," the countess said, "I told them one of my ancestors brought Dr. Faust to Staufen 500 years ago, but that my family had sold the hotel shortly thereafter. I also told them I had no records from that era."

"Is that all?" Tony asked, waving the gun at the three ladies.

They all gasped, "That's it. That's it."

"Are you certain that is all?"

Virginia started to say something about the wine family, "There is . . ."

"That is all," the countess interrupted, cutting her short.

"What were you going to say?" Tony demanded as he came close to Virginia Rufer.

"There is no more. That was it," she stammered.

"I will report this to my padrone and see what fate he wants for you. A telephone. You have a telephone?"

"There is one here," Dimitrios said, "On this table by me."

"Back away," Tony ordered.

Tony picked up the phone and was dialing Sicily when Dimitrios lunged for him. Tony fired at him and hit him in the leg. Then they both fell to the terrace floor and Ridley joined the fray. He knocked the gun away. Tony punched Rid once in the right eye, but, with Dimitrios clinging to his waist, he was no match for Ridley. Rid hit Tony several times in the face in rapid succession.

The countess then leaned over the table and picked up Ridley's gun. She released the safety and fired one shot through the glass door behind the fighting trio. They stopped immediately. Ridley relieved the countess of his gun. He told Tony to lie face down on the terrace.

The countess went to Dimitrios to tend his wound. "You old fool," she said affectionately.

"For you, anything," he replied.

"Donna, go to my bathroom. In the cabinet is a first aid kit. Virginia, get some rope from the garden shed so we can tie up this criminal. Barbara, you call the police and an ambulance."

As they rose from their chairs to carry out the countess's orders, Barbara whispered,"Doesn't he look like Victor Mature?" They all giggled.

While waiting for the police to arrive, Ridley told Tony he would ask that he be charged with breaking and entering, carrying a concealed weapon, and assault with intent to kill. "It will be a long time before you leave Corfu," Ridley said.

"Maybe. Maybe not. We have connections in Greece," he replied.

"You will be here. The lone Italian in a Greek prison. Not a good thing," Dimitrios said.

"Ugh!" was Tony's only response.

"I do think it is a good idea to call your boss. What is his number?" Ridley asked.

"Can I talk?" Tony asked.

"Yes, and then you can turn it over to me."

Tony gave the number while Ridley dialed. When it was answered, Tony said, "Gino, its me, Tony. Get the padrone."

He held the phone until Corleone was on the line. "Padrone, I have trouble. I have been captured at the countess's villa. An American and a Greek overpowered me. Then the countess got a gun and shot at me."

Pause.

"No, I am not hurt. I need a lawyer in Corfu."

Pause.

"Thank you, Padrone."

Pause.

"Yes Sir. The Keenes had been here. She told them nothing. Only that her family had owned the hotel in Staufen used by Faust. But they have no records and are not currently involved."

Ridley took the phone from him and said, "Mr. Corleone, my name is Ridley Taylor. I'm from the American Embassy in Switzerland. I have been working on this case with the Keenes. I can assure you there is no more here to learn. Please call off your people."

Pause.

"Thank you, Sir. I will ask the police here to limit their charges to breaking and entering and carrying a concealed weapon. We'll treat the gunshot as accidental if the countess and her man agree."

Pause.

"Yes Sir."

Ridley handed the phone back to Tony. He listened sheepishly for several moments before saying, "Yes Padrone, I understand." Then he hung up.

He turned toward the countess and implored, "I want to apologize for my behavior. And for shooting your man in the leg. It was not intentional. I will also apologize to the other ladies. I did not intend to frighten them. I have behaved very badly and I beg your forgiveness."

"I will accept some of your apology. But I must wait to see the extent of Dimitrios injury before forgiving you for shooting him. And he must agree. My friends will speak for themselves."

Virginia had returned with the rope. She said, "I'll forgive him. This has been a most exciting day."

In turn, Donna returned with the first aid kit for the Butler and agreed to accept Tony's repeated apology. Barbara had used her own phone to call the police. She too accepted Tony's words of apology. The police arrived minutes later. They took Tony into custody and put Dimitrios in an ambulance. Ridley said good-bye to the four women and accompanied the police to their headquarters to assist in the charges against Rufini.

The police left two armed guards at the villa. It was one of them that answered our phone call. He told us the ladies were all right and that the American had gone with their commander to headquarters to assist in the arrest of an Italian.

We would have to wait to get the full story from Ridley. We decided to go to the hotel dining room for dinner. After a first course of avgolemono soup, we shared a wonderful rack of lamb. We were on our second Ouzo after dinner in the bar, listening to a jazz trio, when Ridley finally walked in at 11:30. He told us the details of the encounter with Rufini and how well the ladies had performed.

"They convinced the Sicilian that all the countess told you was she had no records. They did not reveal the ownership by the Knopfels. That's why I had him call the Don. I wanted him to stay away from Staufen."

"We have taken the liberty, Rid, to have us all booked on the 11:00 Lufthansa flight from here to Frankfurt. We can take a train from the airport to Freiburg. I found Staufen on a map. It's between Freiburg and Basle," I told him.

"Good," Ridley said, "I'll arrange for an embassy car from Bern to be delivered to us at the Freiburg station."

We left Rid in the bar. He had ordered a chicken sandwich and was on his third scotch when we went up to our room.

Once in bed, Lyn said, "We really are doing all right, aren't we, Clark?"

"Better than that. We're probably in the running for the spies of the year award, Honey!"

We laughed and again started thinking about Fran and Beaver Schultz.

"Rudi Heiss must pay," I said as we went to sleep.

Chapter 29

Tuesday, February 26
Day 9, Various

It was raining when I woke up at five minutes till eight o'clock. Lyn was in the shower, which sounded like it was playing baritone to the staccato soprano of the rain against our balcony's sliding glass door. I was again going to have to wait my turn for the bathroom, so I turned on CNN International. Colin Powell and Dick Cheney were holding a news conference. They were describing the progress in the Gulf War as excellent and predicting the liberation of Kuwait within hours.

Lyn came into the bedroom and asked, "What's the news?"

"The war is going very well. We're winning with almost no casualties."

Then I went in to shave and shower. Lyn kept me posted on an interview with General Schwarzkopf about Scud missiles being fired at Saudi Arabia, and the threat of Hussein's using chemical weapons. The general said both were largely ineffective.

We packed for our flight to Frankfurt. We decided to go down to the Dining Room for their buffet breakfast. We weren't sure if we would get anything on the plane.

Ridley was already at a table. "Have you seen the news?" I asked.

"Yes, it looks good for our side, doesn't it?"

"It sure does," Lyn answered.

"I talked with Bryan Roberts this morning. He is at our air base in Wiesbaden. I didn't get a chance to tell you that we had a problem at the Palermo airport Sunday. General Hanfi was killed and Seraph Najim got away to Jordan on our plane. Ken was wounded. They should know his status today. Several police officers and the two assailants were also killed."

"Wow! When will it end?" I mused.

"The war should get the Iraqis out of it. Bryan said reports from the gulf say there is now almost no resistance. They project fewer than 200 U.S. casualties. Get some food and join me."

We loaded up at the buffet with scrambled eggs, cheese, sliced cold meats, various breads, yogurt (none for me), juice, and our usual tea and hot chocolate.

When we sat down, Lyn asked, "Do you think the weather will delay our flight?"

"It's supposed to stop this morning so we should be all right," Rid answered, "I told you Bryan Roberts from Washington was in Wiesbaden. He came over to help with the interrogation of the general. In any event, he said he would meet us at the Frankfurt airport and drive us to Staufen."

"Good," I replied.

"I feel good about our visit with the countess," Lyn started, "I have a good feeling about the lead to the Knopfels. It feels like we are getting closer to an answer to our friends' murderers."

"You are. You two are performing admirably. I'd have you on my team anytime."

"Thanks, Rid. Lyn and I really appreciate your support."

"There have been a lot of us watching after you. Including Bryan Roberts and his team in D.C."

"We'll thank him when we meet him later today."

✤ ✤ ✤ ✤ ✤ ✤

Seraph Najim was arriving in Frankfurt that morning on her flight from Amman. She was traveling under a false Jordanian passport as Sarla Naiit, a dress designer on her way to the trade fair in Frankfurt. She passed through security easily. Then she went downstairs to the train station below the air terminal and boarded a train headed south to Heidelberg.

✤ ✤ ✤ ✤ ✤ ✤

Rudi Heiss had left the Berlin Zoo Bahnhof at 5:34 A.M., due to arrive in Heidelberg at 1:05 P.M. He was about two hours behind Seraph.

We did leave Corfu on time, as the rain stopped as predicted. We landed at 1:10 P.M. We were escorted quickly through customs and taken to a private parking area where we met Bryan Roberts. He was a large, handsome black man whose bright smile made you his friend instantly.

"I've heard a lot about you two," he said, "so much, I feel I already know you."

"We're happy to finally meet you," Lyn said. "We know our lives have been in your hands for several days."

"Not just mine. We have an excellent team on this back in Washington. Plus, Ridley is our best field agent. You didn't hear me say that, Rid," he smiled.

"Remember it at salary time, Bryan," Taylor answered.

During the drive we learned that Bryan had played defensive end at Howard University and had been drafted by the New York Giants. He made it to their final cut, but lost out when the teams financial man, Roy Posen, suggested they could fill that spot on the roster at less expense with a lower draft choice. So Bryan's pro career was a victim of the salary cap.

We discussed the list and our planned visit to the Knopfel winery in Grunern. Ridley suggested we might want to stop and see the professor in Heidelberg, as it was on the way.

"That's a good idea, Rid," said Bryan, behind the wheel. "We go right by Heidelberg. In fact, we should be there in about half an hour."

"All right," Lyn added in her imitation German accent, "Let's see what Herr Professor Schnelling can tell us."

"Yes, maybe he can tell us about the student who wrote the notebook," I said.

Chapter 30

When Seraph Najim arrived in Heidelberg, she went to an address on Neckargemundstrasse. It was a large building converted into apartments for students at the university. She rang the security bell for number 404.

A voice with a middle-eastern accent answered in German, "Ja, Wohl?"

She said in Arabic, "It is Seraph Najim. I believe you were told to expect me."

The reply followed in her native tongue, "Yes. Yes. It is an honor to have such a respected leader visit our lowly place."

"Let me in," the buzzer sounded.

She climbed to the fifth floor and found apartment 404 in the back. The door was being held open by a young Libyan.

"I am Habib," he said. "We have been waiting for you. It is an honor . . ."

She cut him off with, "You said that. Let us do our business. I am in a hurry. The infidels are invading my homeland today, and I have the best opportunity to turn this holy war to Allah's favor."

"Yes, honored one. It is our privilege to help. Ali," he called, "Ali, wake up. Our guest is here."

Another young Arab entered the room, wiping his eyes. He was carrying a paper bag.

He bowed and said, "I believe this is what you have come for."

She opened the bag and removed an old German Luger. It was rusty. "Does it work?" she asked with a look of disdain.

"Yes, I have tested it this morning," Ali said. "It was all I could get on such short notice."

She moved it from hand to hand, felt the weight, smiled, and said, "It has a good feel. How many rounds do you have?"

"I only could get eight."

"And you used one of those?"

"Yes."

"Seven will have to be enough for my mission. Now, tell me about Professor Schnelling."

"He teaches chemistry," Habib started. "He has a laboratory class this morning until 1:00 P.M., then he always has lunch with his assistants at the Red Ox Tavern. After that he is in his office from 2:00 P.M. until 4:00 P.M., according to the sign on his door."

"Where is his office?"

"It is in the Science Building on the road up to the castle from University Platz."

"Thank you. My mission must be kept secret. You have told no one I am here. You did not say what the gun was for?"

"No," replied Ali, "the student I bought it from was drunk and wanted money for beer."

"Good. I need to test this, too." With that, she raised the Luger and shot each of the students once between their eyes. "Now I have five rounds left. It will be enough."

At 2:05 there were three students waiting in the hall when Professor Schnelling arrived and unlocked his office door. He recognized the first two as some of his brightest students. The third he wasn't sure about. She was very attractive, with dark hair and skin.

Probably a foreign student who is considering taking a class in chemistry, he thought. "One at a time, please. Who was first?"

The blond girl, Hilda Braun, was first and wanted him to explain the homework assignment papers he handed out in class that morning.

Next was Steven Hazelrigg, a brilliant pre-medical student from the United States. He wanted to challenge an answer of the previous weeks exam that the professor had marked incorrect. After some discussion, the professor agreed the answer given could also be correct. He said he would change the score to a perfect 100 percent.

Seraph entered the small office and sat across the desk from the professor.

"You are not one of my students, correct?"

"I am not a student. I have a much more important question, Herr Professor."

With that she pulled out of her pack the copy of the notebook and list she had taken from Lieutenant Bazzani in Rome. She had made and mailed one copy to Baghdad before going to Palermo.

"Can you tell me what this is all about? Also, why is your name on the list?"

The professor looked at the list and notebook. As he began to flip through the pages he started to laugh. "I recognize this instantly. The original was stolen from this office two weeks ago. I can assure you it is worthless tripe."

"Go on," she ordered.

"It was the working papers and notes made by a student of mine for his masters thesis several years ago. His name was Franz Biekert. At the time, he was the leader of a student group that was part of a larger neo-nazi movement. The 'Aryan Elite' they called themselves."

"More," she demanded.

"This Biekert actually believed he was going to find the formula for making gold. These notes are mostly about experiments along that line. All preposterous, as gold is a base element. It cannot be made."

"Are you certain of that. Not even with modern technology?"

"Only nature can make gold. And it finished making it several eons ago. Biekert became so distraught over his lack of success, he killed himself by leaping off the castle cliff."

Seraph pulled out her Luger and pointed it at the professor. "One last time, it cannot be done?"

"You don't have to threaten me. I stake my professional reputation on it. I have dabbled with these experiments. Gold can not be manufactured. Period."

The office door opened and Rudi Heiss entered with his Walther PPK aimed at Seraph's head. He was saying, "I'd like for you to repeat what you have told her, Professor. You, put your weapon on the desk," he ordered Najim.

As she leaned forward to comply, she raised out of her chair. Simultaneously, she fired a shot into the professor's heart and she kicked out sideways with her right foot, catching Rudi on his gun hand. Seraph was off balance and her next two shots lodged in the wall beside the door. Rudi spun back and fired at her, grazing her cheek. The pain was searing hot. She jumped backwards, rolled over firing again at Rudi who was lunging behind the desk. She shot again at the torso as it was disappearing. Rudi screamed as he was hit in the thigh. Encouraged by his scream, Seraph rose to her feet, leaned over the desk, pointed at the prone German and pulled the trigger. Click. Click. She had used her five rounds.

She raced for the door. Rudi rose, smiled, and fired again. The bullet hit her in the back and slammed her into the door. Rudi grabbed her and threw her into the chair. She was woozy but conscious and tried to fight him off. He slugged her across the face with his gun. She slumped in the chair.

Rudi then checked the professor. He was dead. He went back to Seraph. She was regaining consciousness.

"What did he tell you?" barked Rudi.

"I will go to Allah before I tell you."

"I think not," he said as he pulled out his stiletto.

Rudi began carving his initials into her face, but she remained silent. He tore open her blouse and cut off her nipples. Still no response. She was becoming weaker and he was becoming concerned that someone might come to the office. He thrust his knife into her heart. Saddam Hussein's search for gold ended with her last breath.

Rudi opened the door to empty hallways. He quickly made his way out of the Science Building and off the campus. He went into the bar at the Hotel Zum Ritter. He ordered a beer and asked the bartender to bring him a telephone. He called Bormann. Max was disappointed in the report that Rudi overheard the professor say that gold could not be made. He was pleased that the Iraqi woman was out of it, however. He asked Rudi about his wound.

"Just flesh, Max. The bullet passed cleanly through my thigh. A little antiseptic and a bandage. I'll be fine."

"Then go on to Staufen and check out this Gunter Siegrist from the list."

"Yes, Max. I'll rest my leg here at the Zum Ritter overnight and go on to Staufen in the morning."

"Gut!" Max said as he hung up. Rudi ordered another beer and asked the barman for directions to the closest pharmacy.

Bryan pulled our car up to the university's Administration Building. We waited while he went inside to get directions.

He came back and said, "We can leave the car here. The professor's office is in that building across the way. He is supposed to be there until 4 P.M."

We walked across the campus to the Science Building, having missed Rudi Heiss limping the other way by no more than ten minutes. We found the office and Ridley opened the door.

"Oh my God!" he yelled, "We're too late." We all crowded into the small room and took in the carnage. "That's Seraph Najim," Rid said. "She's the one that was in Zermatt and Italy."

"Almost got me killed in Palermo," Bryan said, "when Ken was hit."

"That must be the professor," I pointed at the body laying on the desk.

"Looks like Heiss must have been here, too. She's been carved up with a stiletto," Bryan was studying the scene. "There are slugs from this Luger and another weapon here. This gun is empty."

"Looks like she may have run out of ammunition," Bryan said.

"She must have been here first and shot the professor. Then it looks like the two of them had a battle and Rudi won because he had more bullets," Rid explained.

"Too bad," Lyn said.

"You're right about that, Honey. I wish she had killed the SOB."

"We need to get out of here fast," Rid urged. "Let's leave this for someone else to find. We can fill in the locals by phone later. Rudi is ahead of us and I'll bet he is on his way to Staufen."

"Right, Rid. He'll probably go after the Siegrist on the list," agreed Bryan.

"We need to warn him," Lyn said as we left the office.

Soon we were back on the Autobahn headed south toward Staufen and what could be the end of our search.

Chapter 31

Bryan picked up the car phone while Ridley drove us toward Staufen. He made three calls. The first was to Major Wallis. He learned that Willi had left early that afternoon to drive to Staufen. He planned to check into the Gasthaus Zum Lowen and he was holding two other rooms for the Keenes and Taylor.

The next call was to the Gasthaus. The new owner, as of last fall, Wolfgang Strch, answered and went to fetch Willi to the phone.

"Ja?" he said as he came on the line.

"This is Bryan Roberts, Major. I am with the Keenes and Ridley Taylor, just north of Freiburg. We should be in Staufen by 6:30."

"Should I get another room for you? They have only five."

"Yes, Major, please. But the reason I called is that we believe that Rudi Heiss is on his way there ahead of us. He may already be in Staufen. We think he'll go after Siegrist from the list."

"I had asked the owner where I could find Herr Siegrist so we could meet with him. I will do so now and alert the local authorities."

"Good. We'll come straight to the Zum Lowen."

"Okay."

The third call was to Brendan Howard in Washington.

"Hey Bryan, how goes the field work?"

"Not as cushy as sitting where you are. You heard about Palermo."

"Yeah. Too bad you didn't get to talk to General Hanfi, but the war continues to go very well. Less than 120 U.S. wounded."

"That's great B-Man." He went on to fill him in on Heidelberg and asked him to contact the police there.

Brendan told Bryan of Kermit Blackmann's visit with Secretary Brady. They agreed to cooperate. If Faust's list is found, they want to bury it in Fort Knox so it can never be used. Brady is also to ask the president for permission to brief the finance ministers of the large money trading nations. That includes England, France, Germany, Italy, Japan, Russia, and Switzerland. They want them ready to cut off trading if a large new supply of gold starts to flood the market."

"Will the president agree?"

"Apparently there was a drop in the market recently when it was thought a huge new gold field had been discovered in Borneo. Also, the president needs to keep the support of these nations in the war."

Bryan hung up and filled us in on the news.

"Won't Germany make a claim for anything we might find?" asked Lyn.

"I would think they would," Rid said. "Faust was a German and Staufen is in their country."

"Maybe not in the 1500s," I suggested.

"That may be enough for us to sneak anything we may find to Fort Knox. Then the lawyers can argue about it for another 500 years," Bryan quipped.

Lyn put another hat in the ring, "Willi may say it's evidence in his murder investigations."

"I doubt the Germans would let him take it out of the country," Ridley answered. "But, hey, we haven't found anything yet."

"And if we do," I countered, "what's our plan?"

"We sneak it out," Bryan said firmly.

We passed around Freiburg on the E35. Then about twenty kilometers further south at Bad Krozingen, we saw the exit for Staufen. It was only twelve kilometers east where the town sat at the base of the Munstertal range of pre-Alps. Lyn was the first to spot the castle ruins in the twilight as we entered our collective goal, Staufen im Breisgau. I thought to myself, "Dr. Faust, we are here."

We knew a confrontation with Rudi Heiss was imminent. But we were wrong in assuming he was already in Staufen. He was nursing his wound in Heidelberg before he resumed his role as pursuer. His thoughts paralleled ours, that a confrontation with the us was imminent.

Chapter 32

Tuesday, February 26
Day 9, Staufen

We found the Gasthaus Zum Lowen. It's location on the main square made it a natural gathering place for residents and visitors alike. It had a portrait of Faust painted on the outside wall with the date of A.D. 1530 below. The two main streets, Hauptstrasse and Kirchstrasse, were closed to automobile traffic. It was evening so we were allowed to drive up Haupstrasse to the hotel and drop our bags. Then Bryan took the car up past the church to a parking lot.

The weinstube was very busy and the Gasthaus owner and his wife were racing in and out of the kitchen serving their clientele. The owner was a thin, handsome man. He had a mustache and was wearing formal, striped pants, a white shirt with gray tie, and a black vest. We discovered later this was his everyday uniform for serving his guests. He had been the head of all the kitchens in Germany for Hilton Hotels. He retired early to realize his life's dream of owning his own hotel and restaurant. We stood for a few moments at the end of the bar which doubled as the hotel's front desk.

Herr Strch paused briefly in the scurrying to ask if we wanted a table. We pointed to our bags in the foyer and told him we had rooms reserved by Major Wallis.

"Ah, yes," he said in good English as he handed me three room keys. "Here, go on up. You can register later."

He went back to his bar activities. Bryan returned from parking the car and we all started up the stairs.

Ridley and Bryan took rooms 2 and 3, which were on the third floor. Room 1, also three flights up, was apparently already reserved. We took room 4 on the second floor. Room 5 was the only other room on that level. As we paused by our door, after carrying our luggage up two flights of stairs, the door to room 5 opened. It was Major Wallis.

"Welcome," he said. "Welcome to the room of Dr. Faust."

We all went into his room. It had Faust pictures everywhere. There was a glassed-in alcove on one side with lots of test tubes, lab bottles full of colorful powders, and other laboratory paraphernalia on display. Even the large, dark, wood bed frame and headboard had Faust carved into it.

"Do you think this is where he worked?" Lyn asked.

"Pretty small," Ridley said.

"No place to build a fire either," I added. "Wouldn't he need fire, according to what we've learned?"

"No doubt, but remember, this place has been rebuilt," Bryan said. "What's on the other floors, Major?"

"Call me Willi. Everybody does. The ground floor is the weinstube and the kitchen. Plus, there is a small breakfast room in the back. On the first floor there are two private dining rooms. A large one across the front of the inn and a smaller one below room 4. There are also the public rest rooms on the first floor. This floor has only the two guest rooms. The front is open space above the larger private dining room. The third floor has three guest rooms, numbers 1, 2, and 3. Number 1 is the largest in the inn. It has been reserved for Countess Liesel von Anton, whom you met in Corfu."

"What do you suppose she wants?" Lyn asked.

"Protecting the family interest, maybe," I said.

"What about Gunter Siegrist, Willi?" Rid wanted to know.

"The local authorities tell me he is out of town. Been in Strasbourg for the week. Due back Friday. The local chief is trying to reach him to warn him of the danger."

"Let's get unpacked and go downstairs and try some of the good local wine," I urged.

"And some food. I'm starving," Lyn added.

The Knopfel wines were quite good, particularly their Gewurzterminer. Our host, Herr Strch prepared a family style dinner of sauerbraten and large bread dumplings.

We were on dessert of apple strudel and our fourth bottle of wine when Countess von Anton arrived. We were pleased to see her man, Dimitrios, was with her. His leg was in a cast and he was using crutches, but he was still directing the movement of her luggage by the limo driver that had driven them from Zurich.

She came to our table. We all rose to meet her. I introduced Bryan Roberts and Major Wilhelm Wallis, then said, "We heard you were coming, Countess. Is there a problem?"

"I became concerned," she replied, "that I may have put the Knopels in danger. Our families have known each other for centuries."

"I can assure you, Countess," Ridley answered, "we have told no one about the Knopfels. I was with you and your tenants."

"My friends," she corrected.

"With you and your friends when you concealed the Knopfel name so well from Mr. Rufini. Thus, I presumed you wanted it kept secret."

She peered again at Willi and Bryan.

"Excuse me," I said, "for the abbreviated introductions. Major Wallis is the chief of homicide for the Zurich Police and has been investigating the murders in this matter. Bryan Roberts is a senior official with the United States Government. Ridley Taylor works for him. They can all be trusted."

"Gentlemen," she acknowledged.

"We only arrived this evening and have not tried to contact the Knopfels," Lyn said, "We have enjoyed some of their wonderful wine. May I pour you a glass?"

"No thank you, Dear. It has been a long day and I am sure Dimitrios's leg must be bothering him. I think I'll retire. I would like to accompany you to Grunern tomorrow to see the Knopfels. I could call and set it up, if that is all right."

"That would be wonderful," Ridley said.

"Please tell me about Gunter Siegrist. Is he safe?"

"Yes Countess," Willi answered, "I have been checking on him. He is safe in Strasbourg."

"Good night then. I will be at breakfast at 9 A.M.," she said as she left the table.

She made arrangements for Dimitrios to sleep in the porter's pantry behind the kitchen, and began to climb the stairs.

"A most charming lady," Willi said.

"Unmarried, too, Willi," Lyn joked.

We discussed our plans for the next day. We would meet for breakfast at 9 A.M. Willi and Bryan would check with the local chief to see if he had reached Siegrist. If necessary, they would drive to Strasbourg to see what he knew. Ridley, Lyn, and I would accompany the countess to see the Knopfels.

Lyn and I left the three professionals to finish the wine. We started up to our room and paused on the first floor to look into the two private dining rooms. The doors were locked, but we could peer through the stained glass. The smaller one under our room was set up with a large, heavy wooden table like a board of directors would have. The walls were dark wood paneling with family shields hanging all around. It looked like something out of the Teutonic Knights.

The front room was much larger, two stories high. We couldn't see all the way in, but it must have covered the entire front of the building. It was painted an almond color with timbered beams on the ceiling and around the chair rail.

We went on up to our room and both felt exhausted, yet still excited about another day of playing spies.

"I hope the Knopfels will have something to help us," Lyn said.

I thought that would be good, but said, "Don't count on it, Honey. We are looking for something that's been lost for 500 years. It probably burned right here in this hotel with Dr. Faust. One of the pictures on the stairs shows him blowing the place up."

"Well, Clark, I have a feeling about this. I think we're going to find something."

I fell asleep feeling Faust and Mephistopheles would come to me in my dreams offering to lead us to their list in return for our souls.

Chapter 33

Wednesday, February 27
Day 10, Staufen

I was reminded of one of our company's convention breakfasts when we entered the Zum Lowen's breakfast room just before 9 A.M. Countess von Anton was seated alone, with Dimitrios trying to help Herr Strch serve her home canned fruit and hard rolls with cafe latte. Bryan and Willi were at another table conferring with a man in uniform. Presumably the local police chief. Ridley was at a third table talking boisterously with someone we had not seen before. He waved us over to the two empty seats at his table.

"This is my very good friend, Milton Young. He does the same thing I do, but for British Intelligence. MI 6, they call it."

"A genuine pleasure Mr. and Mrs. Keene. I've been hearing a great deal about you from Ridley."

"Nice to meet you, Mr. Young," I offered my hand.

He shook it vigorously and, like the rest of our growing entourage, said, "Call me Milt, please."

"Milt," Lyn nodded.

We sat down and soon had an assortment of breads, jams and cheeses in front of us. I ordered tea and Lyn was happy to learn they made their hot chocolate with milk.

"Milt and I have worked together many times. I was surprised to find him here this morning."

"Your treasury secretary, Brady is it, called our finance minister late yesterday and explained about this chase for phony gold. The ministers of a number of countries are to hold an emergency meeting tomorrow in Bonn. They want to prepare in advance for any possible crisis, should you find this secret of Faust."

"It's probably a wild goose chase," I said.

"I agree," Milt continued, "but my finance minister is the nervous type. He asked me to find out what is going on. I called Washington for Bryan. I got Brendan Howard, who told me you all were here. So I drove most of the night and here I am."

"You must be tired," Lyn said.

"He can stay up longer than anyone on earth!" Rid answered. "We've sat up many nights together watching one thing or another."

"And talking about getting out of this game so we wouldn't have to sit up," Milt added.

"We've planned for the last two years to form our own international security consulting service. We just can't agree on whether it should be called Taylor and Young or Young and Taylor."

"Sounds like a pipe dream," I said.

"True," they both agreed.

We checked with Bryan on his plans for the day. "The major, Chief Oldham, and I are driving to Strasbourg to escort Gunter Siegrist back to Staufen. We'll have plenty of time to find out what he knows. I'd ask Milt to go along, but it would be crowded on the way back. We're going to take the major's BMW."

"Maybe Milt can go with us to Grunern," Rid said.

"We better see what the countess says about that," Lyn suggested.

Milt said, "Don't worry about me. I'll stay here and watch for this character Heiss. Tell me what he looks like."

The major pulled a picture of Heiss from his pocket and handed it to Milt, saying, "Be careful of him. He is extremely dangerous."

"I know the type," Milt replied.

"I'll check with the countess on our plans," I said.

I went over to her table. "May I sit down, Countess?"

"Please, Mr. Keene."

She wanted to know who was the new person with Ridley. I explained and she was satisfied. I told her the other three were going to Strasbourg to get Gunter Siegrist. She said she already knew that, having talked to Chief Oldham earlier. She also said she had talked by phone with Siegrist. He was her age and had been mayor of Staufen in the 1950s. I detected there might have been something between them when they were young. That may have been the real reason she had come.

"What about the Knopfels?" I asked.

"They have invited us to lunch at 1:00 P.M. If Mr. Young is going with us, I need to call them again. I told them there would be the two of you, Mr. Taylor, and myself."

"Mr. Young plans to remain on watch here in town. There is no need for you to change our plans."

"Good. Perhaps your lovely wife can ride with Dimitrios and me. My driver is to be here at 12:45."

"That's fine. Mr. Taylor and I can follow you in Mr. Roberts' car. I'll tell the others and we'll be ready at 12:45."

I went back to our table and explained the arrangements to the others. Bryan gave Ridley his car keys.

"Why does she want me to ride with her?" Lyn wanted to know.

"While she doesn't show it, I think she is truly worried. I got the feeling that there may have been something between her and Gunter Siegrist."

"I can confirm that," Bryan said. "Chief Oldham said they were an item in their school days and again while he was mayor of Staufen forty years ago."

"Love never dies," Rid quipped.

"I've arrived just in time, it seems," Milt grinned.

"You two get serious!" Lyn commanded, "This could be the day we have all been waiting for."

Chapter 34

Wednesday, February 27
Day 10, Strasbourg

Bryan, Willi, and Chief Oldham left right after breakfast for Strasbourg to pick up Gunter Siegrist. Countess von Anton returned to her room. Milt Young, Ridley, Lyn, and I decided to reconnoiter the town.

Staufen turned out to be a beautiful village with well kept homes and businesses. A small river, the Neumagen, ran up the west side of town, flowing towards the Rhine, some twenty kilometers away. Lyn talked about coming back sometime in the spring, as there were rose bushes and wisteria everywhere. The hills were covered with Black Forrest pine. The streets were lined with horse chestnut trees. But the main feature of the town was the castle ruins sitting on top the closest hill to the center.

We walked to the train station about six blocks north of the Zum Lowen. It was a small, one room ticket and waiting area. The schedule showed six trains a day from Bad Krozingen which was on the main Basle to Freiburg line. The narrow gauge tracks ran through Staufen to Munstertal, some ten kilometers up the mountain.

We waited twenty minutes for the train due from Munstertal on its way back to Bad Krozingen. It matched the station. Two yellow and red electric cars with a drivers booth at each end. This train was nearly empty, with only a few shoppers on their way to Freiburg for the day.

Milt decided he would meet each of the scheduled trains to watch for Rudi Heiss. He would spend the time in between watching the hotel and Gunter Siegrist's house on Weiherweg Strasse. We returned to the Zum Lowen to get ready for our luncheon with the Knopfels.

✛ ✛ ✛ ✛ ✛ ✛

When Gunter Siegrist's escort picked him up in Strasbourg, he was excited. He wanted to know more about how Countess von Anton was and looked than he did about Heiss. He looked at the list with their names on it and read the notebook as they drove back towards Staufen.

After about thirty minutes of study, he said, "I'm not sure why my name is on the list. I have a collection of things about Faust and his time in Staufen. Maybe that's it."

"Do you have any of Faust's own notes or papers?" Willi asked.

"No. I just started to collect these things when I was mayor. I thought we could use them to promote tourism to our town. And now it is a big business for us. Many people come in the summer to hear stories about Faust and to hike the trails in the hills above. I have a small display of Faust materials in our tourist office. And I have a booklet I wrote which is sold in the local stores and hotels. But I'm sure I have nothing from Faust himself."

"Too bad," said Bryan.

"Tell us more of what you do know about Faust, Gunter," Major Wallis asked.

"There is not so much to tell that is actual fact. He seemed to almost have been a legend. All of the tales are full of mystery. Perhaps he encouraged that, as he was known as a sorcerer and magician."

"Was he killed in an explosion as I've heard some say, or was he killed by the townspeople?" Bryan asked.

"Can't really say for sure," Gunter answered with a shrug.

"Where is he buried?" Bryan kept on.

"No one knows. No grave was ever found," Gunter replied.

Willi asked, "Was the hotel ever searched for his papers?"

"Many, many times over the years. Even today, people ask for room 5, Herr Strch says. And he finds the room dismantled when they leave."

"Why room 5?" Bryan pressed.

"The one thing that seems to have been passed down for generations is an old room key. It has a wooden lion with Zum Lowen and the number 5 carved across it. On the bottom, someone took a carver's tool and wrote 'Faust'."

Chief Oldham jumped in, "We also think the stories about him with the ladies are true. There is a Faust museum in Knittlingen where he was born. They have official documents which show how he was run out of several towns because of his romantic episodes."

"Even some of that is suspect, Chief," Gunter interjected.

"Wait a minute," Bryan said, becoming frustrated, "you are supposed to be a leading expert on Faust, Herr Siegrist. Yet, every question we ask is answered with equivocation. Did Faust really exist?"

"Yes, that I can say for certain. But what most people know about Faust was the creation of Goethe, who wrote a play about him. Very little is actual fact. Faust was a man of probably shady character who relished fantasy. Smoke and mirrors were his tools. There is not much more I can tell you, other than the stories we all tell the tourists."

"Tell them the one about his using the common letters of his name and Staufen," urged Oldham.

"What's that?" Willi asked.

"It's a story we tell about how Faust got the baron to hire him. Did you know that the symbol for gold in the basic table of elements is *AU*? Faust and Staufen contain those letters in sequence. This coincidence, we say, is how Faust convinced the baron it was destiny that he should succeed in making gold here. Let me show you."

Siegrist took out a piece of paper and wrote:

F	**ST**

$$\textbf{AU}$$

ST	**FEN**

"We sell these pictures all over town. It also comes in plaques and posters."

"Wait a minute," Bryan challenged, "the table of elements wasn't around at the time of Faust. As I recall from my chemistry class, it was developed by someone named Boyle around 1700. He tried to list all the substances that couldn't be broken down further to distinguish them as elements versus chemical compounds."

"I said it was legend, Bryan. Maybe Faust just talked about the common letters of the town and his name. We do sell a lot of posters."

Bryan went on, "The table of elements isn't correct anymore. I think there were originally ninety-two so called elements. Later they added things like Uranium, Plutonium, and some others. And the atomic age showed that elements could be broken down further into atoms, which in turn were made up of a nucleus and electrons."

"That may be today's scientific fact. But there was a great deal of discussion among the scholars of the middle ages about the make up of matter. It goes all the way back to Plato and others in ancient Greece."

Gunter had had enough of Bryan's science lecture. "Who is to say what Faust thought. And, if he was in league with Mephistopheles, maybe he got the information from him . . . Ja?"

"All right," Bryan succumbed, "maybe the devil made him do it." They all laughed.

Then they began to discuss how they would keep everyone safe from Rudi Heiss.

Chapter 35

Wednesday, February 27
Day 10, Grunern

The drive to Grunern was a very short two kilometers. Except for the sign announcing we were in Grunern, I thought we were still in the outskirts of Staufen. Ridley and I had followed the countess's limousine. Lyn sat in the back with Liesel. Dimitrios was up front with the driver. We left the new road and turned into the little village on the old, narrow Staufen-Grunern road. This was the main street through town and right in the center was the Weingut Knopfel. It had a huge, ancient wooden wine press sitting on a stone floor under a high roof set on wood pillars. The sides were completely open. It was over thirty feet long and must have weighed several tons.

Meyer Knopfel was standing by the press waiting for us. He gave Liesel a big hug and welcomed us all to their winery and home. They had set a table in the aging-room among the casks of Kabinett. After a brief tour of the winery, including a demonstration that the old wine press was still used, we returned to the table where several bottles of their various wines had appeared. At that moment, Johanna Knopfel came out of the house kitchen followed by three teenagers. Each was carrying a heaping dish of food. Meyer introduced us all to his wife and children. Liesel embraced Johanna and delighted in scrutinizing the kids.

They had roasted one of their home cured hams, along with rosti potatoes, egg noodles, turnips, and green beans from last year's garden.

We were well into the meal and sampling the delicious wines, when the countess said, "As I told you on the phone, Meyer, these people are investigating some materials they found related to Faust and the Zum Lowen. I told them my family sold the hotel to yours shortly after the fire."

"That's true," Knopfel began. "My family bought the hotel from the baron who brought Faust to Staufen. The story handed down through the generations of the Knopfels is that the townspeople wanted to get Faust out of town and during a march on the hotel, it exploded killing Faust and three local people. The baron had fallen on hard times. The hotel had to be rebuilt and he didn't have the money. Our family was doing well with the wines and we wanted a place to sell them in Staufen. So we bought the place and had it rebuilt. We also bought acreage that we were renting from the baron so he could pay off his lenders."

"Sometime later, a new lode of silver was found in one of the baron's mines," Liesel said, not wanting us to feel sorry for her. "My family invested that money wisely and we became the lenders by starting local banks throughout this area and in Freiburg."

"Was the rebuilt Zum Lowen the same as before?" Lyn asked.

"It was changed some, as we understand it. The family wanted a larger stube for the sale of our wines. So the lobby was eliminated and the bar became the front desk."

"Were the upstairs rooms changed?" I asked.

"Not then. There was one room on the third floor and two each on the first and second."

"But that's not the way it is now," I said.

"No. There was another fire during World War I. My father then did a more major reconstruction, enlarging the third floor so three guest rooms could be up there. The two rooms on the second floor remained. He converted the first floor rooms into private dining rooms, again, to sell more wine. I have the drawings for that reconstruction."

"May we see them?" Ridley inquired.

"Certainly." He called his oldest son, Ruppert, out of the house where they had gone to eat. He asked him to go to the office in the winery and get the file on the Zum Lowen. He returned with a large folder.

"There is nothing in here as far back as Faust. I checked after the countess called. But here are the building plans for the second reconstruction. There are also pictures of the destroyed building after the fire."

Ridley began to carefully study the pictures while Lyn and I looked at the plans.

"Not much left of the original. Looks like only the stone work survived. See." He handed me the picture showing just the foundation and the two story fireplace intact. The rest was a pile of rubble.

"It looks like the fireplace was preserved in these plans?"

"Yes, my father said they go back to the original building." The light went on for all of us.

"Do you think Faust's room 5 was where the second story fireplace is?" Lyn said it first.

"I do, Honey," I said. "Remember that the way they number floors here is to call the bottom floor the ground floor, and what you call the second story is to them the first floor."

"And," Ridley stated, "they number their rooms from the top down. So when there was only one room on the third floor, during Faust's time, it would have been number 1."

Lyn excitedly jumped in, "Rooms 2 and 3 would have been on the second floor."

And then in unison we all screamed, "And 4 and 5 would be one the first floor where the fireplace still stands."

The countess, too, was getting excited, "Oh, let us go look."

"I can't give you permission," Meyer Knopfel said. "As you know, we recently sold the place to Wolfgang Strch. You should ask him."

"We will," I said. "Why did you sell?"

"The wine business has changed. We sell most of our wine to overseas buyers. Particularly to the Americans. We keep a small store in Staufen. The hotel was a small part of our income and Herr Strch made us a good offer."

"Thank you. You have been most helpful," I said.

"Yes. I had a good feeling about this visit," Lyn added. "And thank you for the wonderful luncheon, Johanna."

"It was wonderful to see you again and to see how much your beautiful children have grown," the countess said.

"We thank you for coming," Johanna answered. "I hope you find what you are looking for."

"I must tell you that there are some very bad people who are also looking for the same thing," Ridley started. "They do not know about you from any of us. But public records would show you owned the gasthaus. So, please, be careful. They are ruthless. We will tell Chief Oldham to watch out for you."

"It is our off season and we have been planning a trip to Munich to see our shippers. Perhaps we will go now for a few days," Meyer suggested.

"Good idea," Ridley replied, "this should be over within a few days."

We finished our good-byes and got into our cars for the short drive back to Staufen. When we got back to the Zum Lowen, Herr Strch raced out to meet us. "Your friend, the Englishman, he has been stabbed."

"What?" Ridley yelled.

"Yes. He was found in the churchyard. Stabbed in the stomach. He had lost a lot of blood. They took him by ambulance to the hospital in Freiburg."

I said, "Rudi Heiss is in Staufen."

Chapter 36

Wednesday, February 27
Day10, Staufen

Countess von Anton became very apprehensive when she heard Rudi Heiss was probably in Staufen and had stabbed Milt Young.

"What about Gunter?" she cried.

"We don't know if they are back from Strasbourg yet," Ridley said, trying to calm her fears. "Major Wallis left me his car phone number. Let's go inside and call." They went into the bar area where Wolfgang Strch let them use his phone.

Their arrival, distress, and entry into the hotel was witnessed from across the square by Rudi Heiss. He had arrived on the 1:15 train from Bad Krozingen. There were only three passengers that got off in Staufen. The other two got into a car and drove away on the road to Kirchofen. Rudi started down Haupstrasse toward the center of town. He saw someone following a block behind. When he reached the square, he entered the tourist office to get a local map. He also looked up the address for Gunter Siegrist on Weiherweg Strasse. It looked like he should go two blocks up Kirchstrasse to the church and then go right to Siegrist's home.

When he came out of the tourist office, he walked past the Rathaus to get to Kirchstrasse. He saw the same man get up from a bench on the far side of the square. He was certain he was being followed. Police, he thought. They have found the bodies in Heidelberg. He quickened his pace, even though each step was painful from the wound in his thigh.

At the church, instead of turning on Weiherweg, he entered the church. He found the back door and circled the building through the alley that separated the church from an apartment complex. He peered around the corner and saw his follower leaning against a tree with his back to him. Silently he came up from behind with his stiletto in his hand. Just as he reached Young, a twig snapped under his foot. Milt spun around to face Rudi and he could see the evil in his eyes. Rudi thrust his blade towards Milt's heart. Milt's quick reflex diverted the blow into his abdomen. Two women leaving the church screamed in terror at the sight. Rudi ran from the scene up Winkel half a block to where it turned on to Auf Dem Rampart. This was where the old city walls were in Faust's time. He found a place to hide in part of the ruins of the old wall and there he waited and listened.

He heard police whistles, watched a patrolman race by his hiding place, and then heard an ambulance siren. It came, stopped, while he assumed they were loading his antagonist, and then wailed away out of town. He waited another thirty minutes before walking calmly down the Rampart to where it crossed Weiherweg. There he found the home of Gunter Siegrist, but no one was home. The street was deserted so he decided to return to the main square and come back in the evening. He was on his second beer at the tavern across the square from the Zum Lowen when he saw us arrive in two cars with several other people. He thought he recognized one of the other men from Zermatt. He decided to sit tight and watch.

✤ ✤ ✤ ✤ ✤ ✤

Ridley reached Willi on his car phone. Willi switched it to his speaker, so all of them in the car heard of the attack on Milt Young.

"How is he?" Bryan asked.

"We don't know. They took him to the hospital in Freiburg."

"Did my officers catch Heiss?" Chief Oldham broke in.

"No Sir. He's still at large. One of your men is here at the hotel standing guard."

"Good. Tell him to stay there. And have the other one go to Gunter Siegrist's home to see if he has been there."

"I'll tell them. Where are you now?"

"Actually, we're just north of Freiburg on the A5 near Marckolsheim. We could be at the hospital in half an hour," Chief Oldham said from the back seat.

"We'll stop there and check on Milt. Then we'll all come to the hotel. Should be there around five o'clock," Bryan said. Ridley hung up the phone and told the others the plan.

"I think I'll have tea now," the countess said. "Will you join me, Lyn."

"Yes, but let's have something stronger than tea."

"I plan to, my Dear."

"May I join you," I asked.

"Certainly," the countess said.

"I'm going out to have a look around," Rid said.

"Be careful," I said.

"I will. I won't go far."

Dimitrios stationed himself inside the door of the weinstube. And the police officer was in the foyer. We felt safe. Herr Strch brought a bottle of Brandy to the table with four glasses. He said, "This one is on the house. May I join you?"

"Yes, please," said the countess. "We would like to talk to you about your front private dining room upstairs."

"Are you planning a party?" Strch asked.

"Not exactly," Lyn said.

Chapter 37

Wednesday, February 27
Day10, Staufen

We told Herr Strch about our quest, from finding the list and notebook in Zurich, through our finding of people on the list in Rome, Palermo, Corfu, Heidelberg, and, now, in Staufen. We told him of our review of the Zum Lowen's rebuilding plans that day in Grunern.

"What we want to do is look at the fireplace in the large dining room upstairs," Lyn said. "We believe that was the real room Dr. Faust used. Not your room 5."

"That is true. Meyer Knopfel told me his father set up the display in room 5 for the tourists. You may search all you want in the fireplace. But don't expect to find anything. I had it thoroughly cleaned after I bought the gasthaus last year. We found nothing. But, yes, search. I will get you the key."

Countess von Anton said she would stay in the stube to finish her brandy. She asked that we come back to tell her what we found. Strch returned with the key and went off to serve some new patrons. Dimitrios stayed with the countess and the two of us went upstairs as excited as five-year-olds at Christmas.

Rudi Heiss had seen Ridley leave the hotel and begin his tour of the square. He went into the rest room, while Taylor entered and left his tavern. Then he saw Taylor go up the street towards Gunter Siegrist's house. He thought about following him, but decided to check on us first. He was looking through the stained glass door of the foyer when he saw us going up the stairs alone. He could see the policeman in the foyer so he waited until he went into the bar area to get a drink. Then he sneaked across the foyer to the stairs without being seen.

✣ ✣ ✣ ✣ ✣ ✣

We went straight to the stone fireplace. It looked very solid, but we each took a side and started pushing every rock. The opening was large enough to burn a four foot log, and it was nearly five feet high. I crawled in and started pushing on the stones that went up the chimney. About fifteen stones later, one of them moved.

"Lyn, I may have found it. Get me that carving knife off the sideboard."

She brought the knife and I pried the stone loose. There was a small recess behind the stone. I reached in and removed a very old oilskin bag. It started to crumble to my touch. I stepped out of the fireplace and laid it on the long oak table. Our pulses were racing. We folded open the pouch and removed a leather folder full of papers, There were two additional pieces of paper on top that had not been bound into the leather folder. They looked like some sort of recipe, with directions on one page and a list of ingredients on the other.

"This must be 'The List' of Dr. Faust," Lyn squealed with joy.

"I'll take that!" Rudi said, as he entered the room.

"Oh my God," Lyn cried out.

"No screams," demanded Heiss, as he pulled out his gun and his stiletto. "Back away. Let me have a look."

He poked at the folder and papers with his knife while he kept the gun pointing at us.

"You have been a very big problem, Mr. and Mrs. Keene, since the night we met at the Baur au Lac in Zurich. I felt you knew more than you told me."

"We didn't find the key until you were gone," I said.

"Silence. Just tell me what you have learned and what are these papers."

"You'll have to figure that out yourself, you murderer," Lyn was staring at him in rage.

"Your friends in Zermatt told me very little. I think you will tell me more."

He grabbed Lyn's arm by tucking his gun under his other armpit and was pushing her into the chair at the end of the table. As he moved past me, I lunged at him. I caught him off balance and we slid across the table to the floor on the far side, knocking over chairs as we fell. His gun clattered on the table. He was quick as a cat and far too strong for me. He lifted me by my shirt and put the knife under my eye.

"Enough of that. You will feel this knife again when I have learned all you know."

"Enough of that is right," Ridley said as he came into the room with his gun drawn.

Without hesitation, Rudi threw his knife across the room, catching Taylor's gun hand. His gun fell to the floor. Then the two raced for each other and a real struggle to the death ensued.

While that was happening, Lyn had picked up Heiss's gun and pointed it at him. "Stop!" she yelled. "Stop, or I'll shoot!"

The two disentangled.

Rudi turned to face her and said, "You won't use that. Give it to me."

She said, "For Beaver and Fran," and she shot him through the heart. Then she started shaking and sobbing.

"It's over, Hon," I took her in my arms, "it's over."

"Yes, it's over," Rid said, "except for getting these things to Fort Knox. Then I'll feel you two are safe."

Chapter 38

Wednesday, February 27
Day10, Staufen

Lyn was happy that she had killed Rudi Heiss, but upset at the same time. Had she done something wrong? Ridley Taylor told her that Heiss would have killed them all had she given up the gun. He was threatening her and it was clearly self defense. He would explain it all to the police.

"I think we should hide these papers and not tell anyone we found them," I said.

"Good idea," echoed Ridley. "That way Bryan can take them back to Fort Knox as planned."

"I'll run them up to our room. Are you okay, Rid?" I asked.

"Yes, my hand is cut, but not severely. I'll get the policeman from downstairs and Herr Strch."

I put Faust's papers in our room and returned to the first floor dining room before the others got there. When they arrived, the policeman checked the body.

"He is dead. What happened?"

Ridley explained while Strch bandaged his hand with the kit he brought with him. Liesel von Anton and Dimitrios also entered the room.

"It's all over Countess," Lyn said. "This is the bad man we all have feared. We are safe now."

"Good!" She turned to Lyn. "Mr. Taylor says you shot him."

"That's right. I feel better for our friends now."

"I'm happy for you. And proud for your courage," the countess said.

I picked up the loose rock from the fireplace and told them, "We did find a hiding place inside the fireplace. It was empty, but it must have been the place used by Faust."

"So now the search can finally end," said Strch. "But I think I will hide things there for future guests to find. Ja?"

"Ja," I said, "that would be fun."

I showed him where to replace the rock. We left the policeman and all went back to the stube where Wolfgang retrieved a bottle of Brandy and fresh glasses.

About an hour later, Bryan, Willi, Chief Oldham, and Gunter Siegrist arrived. Gunter went straight to Liesel. She rose and they embraced. They excused themselves to another table. Chief Oldham and Willi went upstairs to take over the investigation after we told them about our encounter with Heiss. Bryan sat down with us and told us Milt Young was going to live.

"They gave him plasma, which saved his life, in the ambulance. He has had extensive surgery to repair damage to his liver and colon. He may have to give up field work. But I talked to him, and he says to tell you he is fine."

We told Bryan about our finding the leather folder. We said we did not tell the others and he could take the materials back to Fort Knox.

"The president will be pleased. I'll bet he will invite you two to dinner when the war is over."

"We don't care about that. We are happy to have avenged our friends."

"I'll pick up those things from you tonight and leave early in the morning for Wiesbaden where I can catch a military shuttle back to Washington."

Herr Strch prepared a light meal of sausages and sauerkraut. We washed it down with beer. After dinner, Herr Strch turned on the television he had behind the bar to the German news station. He interpreted for us that President Bush had held a news conference moments ago to announce victory in the Gulf War. It had taken just 100 hours to win and evict Saddam Hussein from Kuwait. Pictures of celebrating soldiers and civilians filled the screen.

Lyn said, "And we have won our piece of the war too!"

"Yes, Dear, thanks to you."

We decided to retire early. On the way upstairs, Bryan and Ridley waited in the hall while I retrieved Faust's folder and the oilskin bag. I wasn't sure if Ridley noticed that I didn't hand over the two loose sheets of paper. He didn't say anything.

Lyn and I went to bed and made love. We still grieved for our friends, but knew their killer had been brought to justice. And we did our part to win a war.

Chapter 39

Thursday, February 28
Day 11, Various

The next morning when we went down to breakfast, only Ridley Taylor and Major Wallis were there. Ridley said Bryan left around 6 A.M.

"He said to thank you and good-bye. He plans to write you later." He winked, indicating he had not told Willi about our find.

Willi said, "I would like to drive you all to Zurich today. I need to get your statements about the murder at the Baur au Lac. And we should fill in the details on Zermatt and the rest of our activities, finishing here in Staufen.

"That's fine with us," I said, "we can get our clothes and make new arrangements to fly home."

"I'll go along to help with the paperwork, Willi. Okay?" Rid asked.

"Yes. I was planning on you."

We thanked Herr Strch for his hospitality and excellent meals. He told us the countess was checking out and going to stay a few days with Gunter Siegrist before returning to Corfu. He said he would prepare our bills.

"I'll take care of yours," Ridley offered. "We'll let the Treasury Department pay for it."

The drive to Zurich took only two hours past Basle and Olten. We talked about our last visit to Olten and Willi said again he was sorry for the leak in his office. When we arrived in Zurich, Willi went to check with his staff before we started to do our statements.

Ridley said, "What about those two loose sheets of paper. You didn't give them to Bryan, did you?"

"No. I have them in our travel bag. They appear to be Faust's final notes. There is a date on the top that looks like May 1540."

"Why did you keep them?"

"We told a nice priest in Rome, Monsignor Corso, that if we found Faust's formula, we would share it with him. Who knows, maybe it will work on his DaVinci apparatus."

"I'm coming with you," Rid said.

"We were hoping you would," Lyn replied.

Willi returned with our suitcases from the Glarnischerhof and we went right to work. Lunch was brought in and we finished the file after 3 P.M. Willi and the three of us exchanged good-byes and thanks for helping each other. He made us promise to look him up on our next trip to Switzerland.

"I don't think we'll have dinner at the Bauer's Grill though," I quipped. We all laughed.

When we left the station we took a train out to the airport and got on a flight leaving for Rome at 7:00. We called our friend Georgio at the Albergho Senato and arranged for rooms. He also said he would contact Monsignor Corso to set up a meeting for tomorrow. As we boarded the plane, each of us was thinking about gold.

I said, "What if it really works?"

Then Lyn answered with what all three of us were thinking, "Should we keep it?"

"A most interesting question," Ridley mused.

Chapter 40

Friday, March 1
Day 12, Rome

Our appointment was set with Monsignor Corso for 9:00. CNN International was doing a follow-up story on the war. They were showing a press conference with Secretary of Defense Cheney and Joint Chief Chairman Powell describing the magnificent performance of our troops and their new sophisticated weaponry. They switched to General Schwarzkopf in Saudi Arabia, where he was urging continued action inside Iraq to oust Hussein. Then the announcer indicated that President Bush had said no to the invasion of Iraq. They quoted the president as saying, "We have accomplished all of the goals agreed to by the U.N. Resolution. Kuwait is free."

We met Ridley in the breakfast room. He had talked to Milt Young last night. He was feeling much better.

"He told me he has decided to take a disability pension. He wants me to join him in the private security firm we've talked so much about. I think I will. I'm getting too old for this spy business."

"Not us," Lyn said, "We're ready for our next assignment."

"Milt and I talked about you two as a matter of fact. We would like you to serve on our board of directors."

"That's great!" I said, "We'd love to."

"We plan also to ask Monsignor Corso and Countess von Anton. You need high profile contacts to succeed."

"That would be wonderful," Lyn replied. "You also need talent, which you have in abundance. It will be fun working with you. What would we do?"

"A fairly limited role. Besides drumming up business, we would use you as an advisory group helping us solve whatever mysteries we come across. Milt and I along with any staff we might hire would do the field work, so it wouldn't be as dangerous as this caper was."

"Count us in," I concluded.

Monsignor Corso welcomed us heartily to his office. You could tell he was as excited as we were. He said he had set up Leonardo's apparatus up in it's original place in the Cabinet of the Apoxyomenos.

"Here is what we found. We think it is the list of Faust that has been lost for 500 years," I said, as I gingerly handed the brittle papers to him.

He looked at them briefly and at the date on top. "Yes, yes." he said, "this must be it."

I told him how these sheets were separate from all the others which had earlier dates so we believed it to be from Faust's final experiment. He became even more excited as he interpreted the faded writing.

"This page is the directions for the order of compounds and the amount of heat for the transmutation of lead to gold. The second page is the list and precise quantities of the compounds."

"Can we try it on DaVinci's machine?" Lyn urged.

"Certainly, my dear. It will take some time to gather the compounds. Let me show you the apparatus and we can meet again at 9:00 tomorrow morning."

He put the two pages in clear chemical proof plastic sleeves and led us out into the museum. On the second level, just to the left of the Egyptian rooms, was a locked door to the DaVinci rooms. Inside was a large, complex set up of lab equipment.

"We've used a little more modern heat source," the monsignor said as he pointed to an acetylene torch set up like a Bunsen burner. "DaVinci's papers, which we found part of, suggested he needed more intense heat. I will get what's needed and meet you here tomorrow at 9:00."

"Here is something else I'd like you to consider," Ridley said. He went on to explain his concept of the security firm and ask him to consider becoming a director.

"I'm not sure if I can serve as a director," Father Corso replied, "but I could be an unpaid consultant on problems like this. I would enjoy that very much."

He walked us to the front door of the museum, picked up some V.I.P. passes for us to use the next morning and said, "Tomorrow is Saturday. These passes will get you in ahead of the crowd. It will be quiet in here and we won't be disturbed. That is unless we blow ourselves up like Dr. Faust did."

When we left the museum, Ridley called the U.S. Embassy to inquire about Ken Merrill. He found that Ken had been moved to the American hospital in Rome. He said he was going to visit him and would meet us back at the Senato in time for dinner.

We decided to walk back to the hotel past St. Peters and the Piazza Navonna. It started to rain when we reached the Piazza. The artists were quickly covering their work with plastic. We ran on to the hotel and arrived soaking wet.

"I hope this isn't an omen for tomorrow," Lyn said.

"Who knows," I smirked, "maybe Faust will have the last laugh."

Chapter 41

Saturday, March 2
Day 13, Rome

The next morning CNN was repeating the president's news conference saying the 100 hour war in the gulf was over. Saddam and his invaders had been removed from Kuwait and all coalition objectives had been met. As soon as he was off the screen, a variety of analysts began debating whether or not Bush should have sent the troops on to Baghdad to eliminate Hussein.

"They'll debate that for a long time," I predicted.

We arrived at the Vatican Museum fifteen minutes early. We showed our passes and were led directly to the DaVinci Cabinet. Monsignor Corso was already there and his blow torch fire was going.

"I couldn't wait," he said.

"We understand. We are early as well," I replied.

"I have everything from the list, measured and numbered in sequence. I have just started to heat two ounces of lead. When it is melted, we can begin."

We all put on safety goggles that Father Corso provided.

"Please call me Ricardo. After all, we are in this clandestine experiment together. We should act nefarious."

"All right, Ricardo. Nefarious is my best act," Ridley answered.

It took over ten minutes to turn the lead to a thick liquid in the bottom of its crucible.

"Now, in sequence, Lyn, hand me vial number one."

She passed him each of twelve numbered vials as he asked for them. He was continuously looking at Faust's formula. With the last pouring, we all cringed a little, but there was no explosion. We all peered into the crucible and could see that the liquid had changed color. It looked like gold!

"We've done it!" I shouted.

"Yes, it works!" added Ridley.

"We have made gold," Lyn said. "But should we be doing this for ourselves?"

"We could use it to solve the world's problems. Hunger, disease, wars, everything," the priest countered.

"I don't know," I said, "we've been told a supply of gold like this will ruin the world's financial markets. That it could cause the collapse of many nation's economies."

"Surely not if we didn't dump a lot of it on the market at one time?" Ridley said.

"Before we get too far along in curing all the world's ills, shouldn't we find out if it really is gold?" Lyn calmed the three of us with the voice of reason.

"We have assay scales up in our work room," Ricardo told us. "We use them to check new additions to the museum so we can value the gold pieces. Let's cool this down and go check it."

We waited almost an hour for our "gold" to cool. We had poured it into a mold of an old Roman coin. It came out with the picture of Janus on one side and smooth on the other. Janus was the Roman god the month of January is named for. He had two faces, one looking in each direction, looking at the past and toward the future.

"Hey," I said, "While we're at it, we can go in the counterfeiting business, too."

"Oh, Clark, be sensible."

"Remember we are the good guys," Rid added.

"Let's go upstairs," the priest said.

When we arrived in the large work room outside the monsignor's office, he led us to a small table against the back wall. There were the assay tools and scale. They looked like something from a western movie. Ricardo knew what he was doing. He tested our gold piece three times.

Then he turned and said solemnly, "Not even fool's gold. It tests at under four carats. Worthless."

We sighed and Lyn commented, "The world will have to continue it's own struggles, I guess."